'What was that all about?' Cal asked with mock patience. 'I thought I'd paid enough to avoid the nagging wife routine.'

'I just think it would be courteous to offer a few moments of your time to explain to me where you're going. Do you know when you'll be back?' Sara kept her temper with an effort.

'No.' He was abrupt to the point of rudeness, equally irritated by her. 'I'll call you.'

'Why bother,' her voice was saccharine-sweet, 'when Stephen passes on messages so beautifully? I wouldn't want you to waste money on me.'

A malicious gleam in Cal's eyes warned her of further provocation. 'You know, honey, you're beginning to sound like a real wife.'

'I am a real wife.' She didn't care what he made of that, blue eyes spitting fury at him. 'It's a pity I haven't got a real husband!'

A NIGHT-TIME AFFAIR

BY

CHRISTINE GREIG

MILLS & BOON LIMITED
ETON HOUSE   18–24 PARADISE ROAD
RICHMOND   SURREY   TW9 1SR

*First published in Great Britain 1991
by Mills & Boon Limited*

© Christine Greig 1991

*Australian copyright 1991
Philippine copyright 1991
This edition 1991*

ISBN 0 263 76931 3

*Set in 10 on 12 pt Linotron Times
05-9104-48924
Typeset in Great Britain by Centracet, Cambridge
Made and printed in Great Britain*

CHAPTER ONE

SARA ST CLAIR'S chin lifted. Most of the familiar faces bore the stamp of sympathy when they turned in her direction. Silver-blonde hair and china-blue eyes combined in a vision of loveliness, pride lending a certain haughtiness to the exquisite beauty she possessed.

Normally, she would have enjoyed an evening out at Ravenswood, but of late her father had taken to the gaming tables to repair the family fortunes. No amount of arguing could elicit any more than false promises to give up the allure of easy money, and what had started as a desperate attempt to improve their finances was rapidly becoming an addiction. Viewing the predominantly male attendance at the card table, Sara tightened her lips at the sight of Stephen Appleton, a childhood friend, placing a drink at the elbow of a man she hadn't seen before. '*Nouveau riche*,' she designated him with an unusual trace of snobbery. She didn't know which was worse: philistines buying up all that was beautiful to possess rather than cherish, or the fading gentry gathering crumbs from a rich man's table. Restlessness made her eyes burn with inner heat that belied the cool exterior she projected. If she hadn't been a woman, her father would have handed the reins of St Clair's over to her two years ago when hard work could have rescued the stately home from bankruptcy. Now, he was pitting his wits against a carnivore of the first order and hadn't the sense to see it.

Aware of the tension in the room, Callum Grant searched for the source. London had seemed like home—he understood cities—but Hampshire was something else again. The main challenger in the poker game had 'loser' written all over him, maybe that was it. An addict—it always made the more cautious uneasy. Then he caught sight of the woman, a silent whistle of approval drawn from him. The card game seemed mundane all of a sudden.

'That's Sara St Clair,' his assistant, Stephen Appleton, murmured into his ear. 'Wonderful, isn't she?'

'Super,' he mocked, but the amused eyes he flicked sideways were friendly. 'Twenty-four-carat aristocrat?' The American accent was smooth but immediately recognisable. He picked up a card and moved a chip across the table. The amount made those around the table gather closer. 'Who's the guy with more money than sense?' He sat back and spoke in an undertone to the young man next to him. His eyes searched for Sara St Clair.

'Sara's father. And the rumour is, he hasn't got it to lose.'

'Interesting.' Dark eyes ran over the woman's figure as if he were about to make a bid.

'Cal!' Stephen Appleton sometimes found his employer a little too naked in his ambitions. The higher echelons of British society were not used to Callum Grant's smash-and-grab tactics.

'Just admiring the scenery.' The American smiled slowly, showing that he knew what the other man was thinking.

Aware that she was being discussed, and infuriated by the assessing look the stranger was submitting her to, Sara remained distant from the table. Her presence would mean nothing to her father. She had tried to dissuade him before and merely embarrassed them both.

'Georgie must be mad playing with Callum Grant,' she heard Margaret Cairns, a family friend, whisper to her husband. Sara's heart sank as she realised her father was playing poker with a man who regarded the money at stake on the table as little more than small change. Callum Grant was New York's brightest star, a genuine rags-to-riches story. She imagined he'd be every bit as tough and merciless as his reputation suggested.

He was dressed in a dark evening suit, and the white linen of his shirt contrasted dramatically with his dark colouring. She thought there was something vulgar about his deeply tanned skin. Those around him were pallid or had the golden dusting from the ski-slopes that was appropriate for March. Sara guessed at a Latin influence which would probably account for the machismo. She could imagine him on a beach somewhere, undressing every woman who went by with that bold, over-familiar stare. She felt an instinctive dislike, sensing Callum Grant wasn't the type to play by the rules. For some reason the thought unnerved her.

Watching him analytically, Sara saw that he was playing in a rather bored, couldn't-care-less manner. Then her nerves jolted as his eyes met hers and she recognised the glitter of victory there.

'Fold.' The word was quietly spoken but Sara jumped, totally confused. George St Clair was delighted. The American watched his jubilation with detached amusement.

'You had a winning hand!' Stephen Appleton sput-
tered into speech and was silenced by a direct look.
'Oh,' he chuckled as he saw Cal watch Sara St Clair
leave the room. 'That's it.'

'That,' Grant's voice was low and purposeful, 'is
definitely it.'

The gardens were empty. It was a cold, clear night, the
moon a hard silver disc in the sky. Sara welcomed the
harsh flurries of wind cooling her cheeks. Her skin felt
hot, fevered almost. Her shoulders were rigid with
tension. She knew that Callum Grant had been making
some kind of deal with her when he'd laid down the
cards and lost the game. She relived the moment when
those insolent eyes met hers. Every nerve in her body
shouted, 'Danger!' What the danger consisted of
remained intangible, but the feeling persisted.

Silently, she gazed over the neat garden with its
geometric perfection and longed for the order and
stability symbolised there. Yet even that was a sham.
The garden had been rescued from a forest of weeds.
Ravenswood had been built in the sixteenth century
and had originally been called Brinton Castle. The new
name was drawn from the large black birds that
haunted the castellated stone walls. The hotel was half
ruin but enough money had been spent to make the
contrast charming. The warm glow of lights from
restaurant, bar and casino offered a welcome, while
the ruined walls, vulnerable to a chill spring evening,
had a more poetic appeal to Sara's troubled mind. She
heard a peacock and wondered rather cynically if it was
a recording. The past, she knew all too well, was
expensive to preserve. No doubt the romanticised

Ravenswood appealed to the Callum Grants of this world more than the ruined and distinctly shabby Brinton Castle.

Shivering, she viewed the bowed heads of the daffodils and sighed. She was at war with herself. Friends described her as decisive and practical. They were amused when her decorative looks drew out the protective instinct in the opposite sex. Being of such a nature, she found the slow drift towards disaster very difficult to cope with. She wanted to act. Take up the challenge and fight tooth and nail for the home she loved. If St Clair's had to change hands, then she would use her university education and start again. She loved St Clair's passionately, but she accepted that such houses were a great responsibility and could have borne the loss had it just been herself to suffer. It was her father she feared for; he was too old to change and she knew the loss of the family home would kill him. The desperate need to keep the house had driven him to gambling and put him at the mercy of sharks like Grant.

'Sara?' Stephen Appleton appeared at her side with a shawl. 'You'll get cold.'

She gave him a dismissive look and he silently put it around her shoulders.

'I haven't seen you lately. How are you?' He sounded overbright, and she laughed softly but with unmistakable contempt.

'Doesn't he deign to chat up women on his own? Really, Stephen, I suggest you chase sticks in future, you might have more luck.'

Being compared to an obedient spaniel was not a flattering image but the young man appreciated her spirit. 'I can't think what Cal finds so fascinating. You always were too big for your boots.'

She smiled narrowly. 'Thank you for the shawl.'

'My pleasure.' He bowed in an extravagant fashion, his blond hair almost as fair as hers, but his eyes were grey whereas Sara's were a startling blue.

'What does he want?' she asked as he fell into step beside her. 'If he's expecting gratitude, I'm afraid he'll be disappointed.'

Stephen Appleton shrugged with a man-of-the-world cynicism that sat uneasily on his youthful shoulders.

'He could always go back to the table. At the moment he wants someone to talk to.'

'You talk to him.' Her eyes flashed blue lightning around his head. 'As far as I know, my father has yet to put me up in place of stake money, and I won't be bought!'

'OK, OK.' He held up his hands. 'It's your funeral.'

He fell back, watching her as she walked away. He heard the snap of a twig and looked behind him to see the glow from a cigar.

'She said——'

'I heard.' He joined his messenger, drawing on his cigar, his eyes alive with challenge. 'Think she meant it?'

'Yes.' Stephen Appleton had mixed feelings about his employer's intentions. Despite their verbal fencing, he liked Sara and admired the fact that she was unimpressed by Grant's money, even though he coveted it himself.

'You've got a lot to learn about people,' Cal growled with a lazy purr. 'She just needs the right proposition.'

Stephen Appleton stared at Callum Grant, his curiosity lit. 'What sort of proposition?'

The smile lingering about the American's lips was secretive. 'That's between the lady and myself. Go and enjoy yourself,' he dismissed the man, content to breath in the evening air and smoke his cigar. Time, he felt, was on his side.

'Hello.' Angela Carter leant over her horse's neck and ruffled his mane. 'Where did you disappear to last night? Your father was on a winning streak.'

'So he told me.' Sara's smile was unconvincing.

'I don't expect Callum Grant loses very often.' Her friend gave her a sideways grin. 'Unlucky at cards—you know what they say.'

Sara led her horse Bunter out of the stable and hoisted herself into the saddle. The smell of horse and leather was comforting and familiar.

'I don't expect he loses much at anything,' she muttered. She had the sneaking feeling her father was being fattened like a turkey for Christmas, destroying her anticipation of the drag hunt scheduled for that day.

Despite the fact that the hunt traditionally gathered at St Clair's, she never rode when the quarry was a fox or a hare. She had witnessed a kill when she was still a child and had never got over it. Her friends teased her about it but she hated the idea of killing for sport. Personally she thought the laying of a scent over interesting countryside gave a far better ride, but she knew she was in the minority in that opinion. The others missed the thrill of the chase.

'He must be loaded.' Angela was loath to leave the subject of Callum Grant. 'You could do worse.'

Sara rarely showed anger, but the remark annoyed her. 'I don't know what you mean. Besides, I should imagine marriage is the last thing on Callum Grant's mind; he's not the type.' She dug her knees into her horse's sides. 'And I wouldn't care if he were.'

'Gosh, I would,' Angela mimicked their schooldays. 'You don't often find a hunk with money. He's definitely interested, Sara, he couldn't see the spots on his cards for looking at you.'

Sara discontinued the conversation by urging her mount forward, outdistancing her companion who was happy to plod along in her wake.

The courtyard at the rear of St Clair's displayed a wealth of horseflesh and colour. A sprinkling of red coats and top hats distinguished the few who wore the hunt button. The women were more restrained in black with cream jodhpurs, the children of riding age milling around in their plain ties and hacking jackets. It was the England much portrayed on the big screen and TV serials. Sara found the ritual of the hunt unremarkable; it had been part of her life for as long as she could remember. She nodded to the Master of the Field. Sir James Carpenter touched his hat and smiled; he was her godfather and often teased her about her squeamish reaction to a live hunt.

Out of the corner of her eye Sara saw Callum Grant sitting on the bonnet of a Range Rover. Casually dressed, he looked as if he were posing for a fashion advert. She had the distinct impression he was watching her. She took the traditional glass of sherry and sipped it, trying to disguise an uncharacteristic prickle of awkwardness that his presence brought.

Hours later, mud-spattered and invigorated, Sara dismounted and handed the reins to a pair of waiting hands, shaking her hair free from the confines of her hat.

'I feel better,' she breathed.

'Shame expending all that energy if you didn't.' The lazy tones penetrated her moment of physical and mental peace. 'If you need exercise, I could help you with that. There's a gym at my hotel,' Callum Grant continued blandly, the glare she sent him spoiled by the hair that blew across her face. Silently, he handed back the reins and walked with her as she led Bunter back to the stables.

He introduced himself without making a notable impression. 'You're Sara. I met your father last night.'

'So you did.' She entered the stable and set about removing the horse's saddle. He leant against the wooden door, watching her as she heaved the leather from the horse's sweating body. Her cheeks were flushed and the seconds ticked past without further conversation.

'Take off your jacket,' he suggested, the tone of his voice sounding incredibly intimate. 'You're too hot.'

Ignoring him, she took the horse brush and began to remove the worst of the mud from Bunter's coat.

'You're making it hard, Sara.' His voice remained quiet but it threatened at the same time.

'What's that, Mr Grant?' She bent, checking the horse's legs for cuts and thorns. 'Steady,' she crooned as Bunter moved restlessly. Flicking a barely polite glance in his direction, she decided to be blunt. 'I gave your dogsbody my answer last night. I'm flattered you should choose to speak to me in person.' The sarcasm was barely camouflaged. 'But I'm really not interested.'

'Let's talk about that.' He was maddeningly persistent, and when she straightened she gave him the benefit of her attention. He was regarding her with a certain amount of indulgent humour.

'No!' Her answer was uncompromising.

'We could discuss it tomorrow, but then your father would know his little girl had traded her—freedom to keep a roof over his head.'

Hands on hips, she regarded him with loathing. 'What are you talking about?'

'A game of cards,' his dark eyes wandered over her insolently, 'that isn't going to go his way.'

She subjected him to a similar appraisal. His long legs were encased in black denim. A thickly knit jumper and leather jacket made him look powerfully masculine. The uniform tweed and green Barbours that usually adorned her male friends suddenly struck her as desirably civilised, if a little lacking in vitality.

'I get what I want, Sara.' His eyes clashed with hers as she finished what she hoped was an equally insolent appraisal of his attributes.

'Am I to take it that I come into the category of things you want?' Her voice held the faintest hint of a tremor.

The appearance of a russet-headed youth broke the tension momentarily.

'Make sure he gets the bran,' she instructed the lad who looked after Bunter. He was a boy from the village who was besotted by horses and couldn't afford one of

his own. 'You can take him for a gentle ride tomorrow.
Only half an hour though—promise?'

He grinned and she smiled, hoping that if she ignored
him Callum Grant would take the hint and leave.

'I'll pick you up at seven-thirty,' he said as if her
refusal had never been spoken. 'We'll be dining at
Ravenswood. Be ready, I don't like to be kept waiting.'

Sara watched him go, her eyes hectic.

'Is he bothering you, Sara?' Young Wayne Harrison
also sensed the power of the adult male.

She smiled at him in a teasing manner. 'I can look
after myself. And wasn't it you I saw chasing Jenny
Buchanan?' She laughed at his sudden embarrassment.
'Men,' she observed darkly, 'have a habit of bothering
us poor women.'

Bravado, she observed later, was all very well, but
Callum Grant did bother her. She got the distinct
impression that to follow her instincts and refuse to
dine with him would prompt him to wreck her father's
finances and dictate his own terms. What he didn't
understand was that the St Clairs couldn't be bought.
Ruined, she faced the fact, but not bought.

Sara's pride was pricked later that afternoon when she
caught sight of her father in the study poring over a
pile of unpaid bills. He looked old and unhappy, she
realised with a shock. She had become used to thinking
of her father as weak, not realising how much of his
personal anguish he hid from her.

George St Clair, unaware of being watched, reached
out for his wife's picture, and a lump came into Sara's
throat. Her mother had died when she was eleven. Too
wrapped up in her own pain, she had never really

understood what Katherine St Clair's death had meant to her father.

Biting her lip, she went to her room and telephoned Callum Grant's hotel suite as an act of contrition. She didn't get through to the great man; Stephen Appleton took the message. Despite his excuse that his employer was busy, she guessed Grant was playing with her. He wasn't a man to accept refusal; had she not called, she received the impression that he would have arrived at seven-thirty and severely embarrassed her had she not been ready. The knowledge didn't endear him to her.

Sara dressed with elegance for the evening with her tormentor, but hardly made a great show of her attributes. The golden caramel dress, with full sleeves and an embroidered bodice, was attractive but subdued. It was the sort of dress a smart businesswoman would wear to ensure she looked chic but was also taken seriously. A gold necklace and matching earrings drew attention to the graceful line of her neck and delicate curve of her ears. It never occurred to Sara that covering up in such a manner was likely to fire the male imagination, whereas a more revealing dress would soon assuage it.

Callum Grant arrived in a spray of gravel as he parked his car with a flourish. Her dislike increased when she contemplated the chore of raking it back into its usual smooth perfection. She hurried to her father's study, eager to keep the two men apart. She didn't want any talk of a re-match at the gambling tables to add further pressure to an already difficult evening.

The American was sitting in one of the comfortable armchairs talking easily with George St Clair about his impressions of the hunt. He turned his head as she entered, surveying her leisurely, continuing with his conversation.

'You look nice,' he deigned to acknowledge her, making her perfectly aware that 'nice' wasn't on his list of desirable qualities.

'Thank you.' She pretended to be flattered. 'Shall we go?'

'Have a nice evening.' George St Clair glanced from one to the other curiously, probably wondering why she hadn't told him the friend she was to spend the evening with was the New York business magnate. Sara kissed her father's cheek and walked past Callum Grant without a word. She allowed him to seat her in his Mercedes sports car. It was black and gleamed darkly in the light from the porch.

'I'm glad you decided to be sensible.' He wasn't averse to rubbing salt in the wound.

She jerked around in her seat, and then shrank back as she realised how close they were. He watched the changing expressions on her face with interest.

'Get used to being with me. It's going to become a habit.'

'Not if I can help it.' She felt extremely claustrophobic in the small space and wished he'd start up the car. He rested his arm along the back of the driver's seat.

'You're out of your league with me, sweetheart. I admire spirit, but too much could get irritating.'

'That would really worry me if I cared one atom for what you think,' she snapped, reaching for the doorhandle.

Callum Grant fired the ignition, preventing her from leaving as the car moved forward and she was flung back into the seat.

The dinner was excellent but Sara barely touched
hers. She had chosen a mixture of avocado and pink
grapefruit to begin with and pushed it around the shell-
shaped dish she had been given. He, she noticed, had
little difficulty with the smoked salmon. Studying his
long, square-shaped fingers, she thought he was a little
at odds with the delicate china and silver provided by
Ravenswood. Callum Grant, she mused, needed feeding rather than to have his appetite teased and tempted
by the delicate morsels put before him. She watched
the avocado disappear and be replaced by baked trout
without much enthusiasm.

Presumably having a reluctant guest at his table did
nothing to diminish his appetite. He consumed the
ragout of beef he was served with, the conversation
sparse as he concentrated on his meal. She wondered
if this was a regular occurrence, but, surveying his dark
good looks, she suspected he would have little problem
attracting female interest.

By the time the orange sorbet arrived it was clear
that something or someone had killed her appetite.
Sitting back with a glass of wine in his hands, Callum
Grant studied her with embarrassing intentness. She
fidgeted, looking away, and even made a preparatory
stab at the sweet, then put the spoon down with a
clatter and met his gaze with more bravery than she
felt. Around them bright chatter rippled in waves, the
subdued movement of the waiters hardly registering.

'You're being a little hard on the chef, honey,' he
provoked her mercilessly. 'I mean, if it was me having
a hard time with the food, they'd put it down to an
uneducated palate. But Sara St Clair——' He whistled
silently. 'The guy will probably shoot himself.'

'If you're still hungry, you can have this,' she offered with lashings of condescension, but the glint in her eyes suggested it might adorn his immaculate dinner-jacket rather than his plate.

Something hard and challenging in his gaze got to her. The impulse died.

Beckoning the waiter, he signed the bill and stood up. She followed suit, allowing him to guide her into the lounge area.

'Shall we get down to business?' He took out a thin cigar. 'Do you mind?'

'Yes.'

He unwrapped it and took his time lighting it.

'What business?' she prompted, her irritation evident.

'It's common knowledge among your friends,' his eyes mocked her, 'that George St Clair is as near broke as makes no difference. He's reckless and he's going down. Shortly the house will be possessed to repay debts and you'll be looking for new accommodation——'

'That's hardly your concern!' She was indignant.

'I'm concerned.' He indolently surveyed her delicate features. 'I'm also looking for somewhere like St Clair's to use for business conferences, entertaining. It's suitable. If you agree to my proposition, you can keep the house without any financial overheads.'

She laced her fingers and supported her chin. 'Proposition? I won't be your mistress, so let's not waste time discussing it.'

He smiled at that. 'I'm a practical man, I don't buy houses for the women in my life. I'm expanding into the UK; the old-boy network here is tough to crack.

No amount of money is going to hide the fact that I've worked with my hands and I look uncomfortable in suits.'

She detected a faint hint of resentment in his voice but his face revealed little.

'I don't really understand.' She frowned. 'If the house goes on to the market, you can bid with other interested parties.'

'I want the house with you in it,' he returned smoothly. 'I need a wife and you fulfil the requirements.'

Sara's eyes widened with shock. Then she laughed. 'Mr Grant, you are——'

'Cal,' he said firmly. 'I'd like to hear you say it.'

She blushed. 'Look, I think this has gone far enough. I'd like to go home now.'

He considered this and nodded, getting up and assisting her from her seat. 'I'll give you time to think about it.'

'I don't need time,' she assured him. 'I'm afraid your offer is totally preposterous, and I can quite easily see why you find it difficult to get on in English society.'

He stiffened and looked down at her. 'You can?' He raised an eyebrow but his eyes were hard.

'Not everything is up for sale, Mr Grant. Perhaps you could use your money to employ someone to teach you some manners.'

He opened the door for her and ushered her outside. Stephen Appleton appeared and murmured something in his ear. He nodded, giving him the car keys.

'See Miss St Clair home,' he instructed, and turned on his heel without another word.

'Charming.' She walked towards the car and waited

patiently as Stephen opened the door and saw she was comfortable.

'I recognise that look,' he chattered whimsically. 'Whatever have you said? He's as mad as fire.'

Sara's elation was short-lived. When they turned into the drive of St Clair's, an ambulance was pulling away from the house. A premonition hit her and she scrambled out of the car and ran to the housekeeper, Mrs Pagett.

'I think it's his heart, miss,' she sniffed, her eyes red.

Stephen Appleton obligingly drove her to the hospital. He stayed long enough to assess the situation and then reported back.

Callum Grant listened, undoing his cufflinks and throwing them on the dresser. 'Has she got a close friend, preferably female?'

'Yes, Angela Carter. Shall I give her a ring?'

'Do that. And I want everything you can get on George St Clair.' Undoing his tie, he released the top button of his shirt. 'And, Steve—be discreet.'

'Gotcha, boss.'

'"Yes, sir" will do.' He was abrupt. Flinging his tie down, he looked driven by pent-up energy. 'And get the best doctor there is for the old guy. I don't want St Clair on my conscience.'

Nodding, Stephen Appleton left.

CHAPTER TWO

'HAS anything been worrying your father?' The consultant's question had made Sara face a painful reality. The many problems of maintaining St Clair's had become too much for George St Clair. She suspected the loss of the house that had been in the family for generations would be the final straw.

It made her start with surprise when, on leaving the hospital a week after her father's heart attack, she found Stephen Appleton at her side, handing her an envelope.

'What's this?' She had expected some move on Callum Grant's part but bristled at his use of a go-between.

'Too long to be a love-letter. Believe it or not, Sara, he keeps his intentions where you're concerned very much to himself. All I know is that he's rather determined to further your acquaintance.' Grey eyes gleamed with amusement. 'In fact you're the first woman I've known to put up a fight.'

'I shall take that as a compliment.' She took the envelope and walked to her ancient Morris Oxford. Stephen Appleton dropped back and she glanced over her shoulder to see him enter the hospital. Checking up, she surmised. Her eyes kindled. Callum Grant knew her father's health was his trump card.

When she got home, she went into her father's study. The study-cum-library had always struck her as a sober place, with its dark wood panelling, shelves of leather-bound volumes and heavy red velvet curtains. A massive captain's chair held pride of place. Several silk-covered sofas had been introduced to tempt the reader but the austere atmosphere prompted the bookworm to seek the light and greenery of the conservatory. Sara felt the atmosphere suited her purpose and opened the package, her interest intensifying when a document fell out together with a set of architect's drawings. The document turned out to be a detailed file on Grant's plans for St Clair's. Attached was a draft of a legal undertaking putting the house up as collateral for a substantial loan. Upon the birth of her first child, the loan was cancelled and the house entailed to her heir with a stipulation that the child should be the product of her marriage to Callum Grant and no other.

Sara sat back, stunned. Although she had been expecting something of the kind, to see the proposition drawn up so meticulously made her feel cold. Locking the papers in a drawer of the desk, she poured herself a small measure of brandy and sipped it slowly, keeping her mind deliberately blank. The clock ticked into the silence of the room as if marking her last seconds of freedom. When the hour chimed, she picked up the phone and dialled Ravenswood.

After getting through the grilling given by the switchboard, she heard Callum Grant's smooth, deep voice say her name.

'You've read through everything?'

'Yes.' Her tone was stiff. If he could have seen her pale face and shadowed eyes, he would have appreciated the level of control she was exercising.

'And?' He didn't bother to sell her the idea.

'I have no choice.' She was bitter.

'That isn't an answer.' His voice was hard and unsympathetic.

'Yes, damn you!' She put the receiver down with barely suppressed violence and hoped the noise made him wince.

The next day an auditor arrived but there was no sign of her suitor. Sara had expected him to call round the night before. If it hadn't been for the efficient young man in a pin-striped suit, she could have been persuaded she had dreamt the whole thing.

David Bresslaw was surprised to find the books in such good order and she took great pleasure in presenting him with the mound of unpaid bills.

'Cal will improve things,' he promised, his eyes shining with confidence. 'Don't worry, he'll have this place paying for itself in no time.'

'I'm sure.' She was insouciant. Callum Grant, for all his social disadvantages, seemed to present a heroic image to ex-public schoolboys.

David Bresslaw was a close-cropped, curly-haired man in his mid-twenties. He viewed Sara's white, fleecy jumper and figure-hugging jeans with reluctant admiration. He preferred women in dresses but she was a pleasure to look at.

'Do—er—do you work here, Sara?' he stumbled into speech, a flush spreading over his cheeks at her haughty regard.

'I help run it, yes.' She was well aware of the effect her blonde, blue-eyed beauty had on the male of the species. 'Ring Mrs Pagett if you want tea.'

* * *

'Mr Grant, miss,' Mrs Pagett informed her expressionlessly. There was gossip in the village about the American's interest in Sara St Clair. The housekeeper had staunchly denied any relationship beyond a dinnerdate, but tongues wagged.

The young woman looked up. She was in the small parlour, her own special room, which her father had given her when she reached her teens. It was a clutter of objects and pictures with a haphazard style that came from an artistic nature. She was sitting on a sheepskin rug, her knees curled under her, her father's Labrador sleepily appreciating the flames from the log fire and the stroke of the woman's hand. The fire reflected its warm glow on to Sara's face, her eyes dark blue, her hair almost Nordic in its fairness.

'Thank you, Mrs Pagett,' she dismissed the woman, staying where she was. Welcoming him, she decided, didn't come into the deal.

'I have the feeling compromise isn't in your dictionary.'

Callum Grant came to stand near her, looking down on her bent head as she pretended to be absorbed tickling the dog's ears. Grey cords clothed strongly muscled legs and she was uncomfortable with the proximity. When he knelt down beside her, she shifted restlessly, her eyes meeting his, startled.

He was wearing a black wool shirt, open at the throat, showing tanned skin and a smattering of dark hair. There was something extremely potent about his masculinity and she held her breath as the tang of his aftershave gently teased her senses. Her expression told him he wasn't welcome and he smiled, his eyes warm with an emotion she didn't like.

'I don't think George wants to see little Sara sold to the highest bidder.' He reached out, stroking the back of his forefinger along her jawline. 'But if you want it that way, I'll write and tell him details of the wedding.'

Silently, she maintained his gaze, her hostility apparent.

'If not——' Dark eyes rested on the soft pink of her lips and his thumb pressed gently against the full lower curve, his dark face drawing closer. The heat of the fire against her back prevented her retreat. 'If not, you'll have to be more co-operative.'

Desperately she tried to escape, to find herself ruthlessly manhandled and spread out on the rug. Blue eyes spat her fury at him.

'Why me? You don't even like me!' She tried to release her wrists that were imprisoned above her head. The clichéd role of female surrender enraged her.

'You have possibilities——' he was laughing at her, aware of her feelings '—like this house. You need a bit of work, that's all.'

'I don't want your filthy hands on me. Get off!' she almost shouted. 'If we've made a deal——' She dried up as she remembered what he'd said about her father. He saw the knowledge dawn in her eyes and smiled with infuriating patience.

'There are many kinds of humiliation, Sara. Publicly, we can make it clear that we like each other's company, that we are drawing closer together. People may think you've got yourself a good catch but you won't be thought any the worse for that. That's what girls like you do, play at something until the right man comes along.' He enjoyed her fury. 'Have the requisite number of children to send off to boarding-school and

spend the rest of your life breeding dogs and breaking
the back of some poor horse.'

'Unlike you,' she hurled back at him. 'Wanting to
marry into the upper crust, presumably have the
requisite heir to make sure your investment doesn't go
astray, and then, no doubt, while your time away,
making money and escorting other men's wives.'

'Not if you keep me at home.' He smiled down at
her, his white teeth seeming predatory to Sara's
incensed gaze. 'Shall we practise that?'

Sara's reply was very unladylike and he actually
laughed.

'I think I'm going to enjoy working on you.' His lazy
appraisal made her feel hot. For once she was stuck for
something to say. Suddenly, she was very aware of his
fingers entwined with hers and the pressure of his
weight as he sat astride her stomach.

'Well, what do you want?' he asked, suddenly
serious. 'An invitation through the post, the same as
the other guests?'

'No.' Her admission was soundless; only her lips
moved in denial.

Anger had anaesthetised her to the enormity of the
step she was taking. It was an exhausting emotion and,
although not depleted, Callum Grant's superior physical force eroded its power to protect her. This was the
reality of their pact; her compliance to his unwelcome
sexual demands.

'You'll get used to making the right decisions,' he
deliberately provoked her, his eyes on hers as he eased
his body from a sitting position until he was above her,
his hips very deliberately settling into the saddle of
hers.

Swallowing drily, Sara looked away, her cheeks pink. He moved against her and she quivered with shock at the intimate message his body gave hers.

'You're disgusting!' she accused him hotly, only to have her breath cut off as his mouth fastened on hers. The kiss was one of clearly stated possession. Releasing her hands, he used one arm to support himself, his free hand cupping her face with his fingers, roughly coaxing her into allowing him access to the moist recess of her mouth. Her lips were crushed and caressed by his until her teeth parted and with a smothered moan she felt his tongue glide into her mouth.

Sara trembled with a host of conflicting emotions. She wasn't used to being so roughly handled; she had bestowed what favours she had given and retreated when her admirers became overheated. She had never felt real desire or been a victim of unvarnished male lust. The fact that Callum Grant undoubtedly knew how to kiss didn't make the experience any easier to handle. At twenty-three, she supposed, her body had primitive needs that civilised codes of behaviour couldn't quite subdue. Whatever it was, her mind staggered at her reaction to the two hundred pounds of pure male straining against her. Her toes curled and a restless surge of longing flickered through her blood. Her movement against his imprisoning hips almost invited the hard pressure that forced her back against the rug and punished her with an exhibition of male power that made her stomach somersault in nervous reaction.

The mouth against hers relented a little and his tongue moved teasingly over her lower lip before plunging deeper and seeking the soft touch of hers.

Sara's jaw shook with tension and he withdrew, placing soft kisses around her mouth, the unfamiliar scrape of his jaw chafing her skin.

'I think we're going to work together on this one,' he observed lazily, stroking a tendril of hair away from her mouth and tracing the swollen curves. She looked sulky and rebellious but her eyes showed the embers of passion and they both knew it.

'Play your sort of game long enough,' he told her softly. 'You always meet someone who plays better. I,' he assured her with quiet menace, 'don't play at anything. We'll have a few ground rules so if you get out of line you deserve what you get.' She remained quiet but her eyes told him to go to hell. 'Bad start,' he breathed against her throat, and she closed her eyes, her lips parting.

'All right,' she whispered shakily, unable to bear the clamour of her senses.

'Pity.' His mouth opened against her skin and she stiffened, squeaking with outrage and rubbing the red patch on her throat when he moved away from her. 'These are the rules.' He watched her get to her feet and regard him defensively. 'You save that shrewish temper for when we're alone. In public we're going to act like any other couple about to get married.' He advanced on her again. 'Break the rules,' he slapped her hands away as she tried to push him back, 'and I'll teach you all they forgot to teach you at finishing school.'

'You're an ill-mannered thug.' She couldn't help herself, but then she lowered her lashes.

'You're getting the idea.' He stroked her hair absent-mindedly and bent to press a kiss against her forehead.

His fingers gripped her neck as she took a step backwards.

A knock at the door heralded Mrs Pagett with a tea-tray and they turned in unison, still in close proximity. The American's eyes were bold; Sara looked as flustered as she felt.

'Tea, how nice,' he drawled hatefully. 'Thanks.'

A brief nod from Sara told Mrs Pagett she was all right. Sitting down in a chair, she accepted the tea he poured for her, watching his every move.

'By the way, I hate tea.' He went over to the hearth, resting his arm along the mantelpiece. He looked big and alien in her private room and the fact that he expected her to observe his preferences was a novelty for Sara. That he guessed this was written in the aggravating glimmer of amusement in his dark gaze. Toughness was written all over him, from the broad strength of his shoulders to the aggressive way he stood, his regard direct and unflinching. There was something undiluted about him. Callum Grant was the iron fist without the velvet glove.

'I'll need a list of your social engagements.' His voice broke into her thoughts. 'I'm a busy man; if we're going to see each other over the next few weeks I'll have to rearrange my commitments.'

She pointed to a small diary on the table and continued to view him over the rim of her teacup.

'Good.' He picked it up and pushed it into the back of his jeans. 'Do you need any money?'

The look she gave him was poisonous. 'I'd rather starve.'

'Nice to know one of you is going to be—economical.' The word 'cheap' was made even more pointed by its deliberate omission.

'Goodnight,' she bade him coldly.

'Sweet dreams.' He blew her a kiss and left.

Sara seethed silently; she had seen the smile curving his mouth as he turned away. She hated Callum Grant more than anything in the world. What was worse, he knew it. So why did he want this marriage so much? A host of aristocratic beauties would fall for his looks and money. It wasn't as if he was a social embarrassment—his self-confidence was colossal and his ego didn't lag far behind. Why did Callum Grant want her? It was a puzzle she was unable to solve.

Easter Saturday saw the grounds of St Clair's open for the village fête. The house was out of bounds, a natural boundary of clipped juniper trees fortified by bunting indicating the perimeter of the event.

Children were running around the maze, the possibility of not being able to get out making them shout to each other and giggle. In fact the maze was designed so that the likelihood of their arriving back at the entrance was the greater possibility. It took skill to find the centre. Workmen were busy stripping part of the roof that needed repairing. Callum Grant's money had already begun to make substantial improvements to St Clair's. The family had been putting off repairs for years.

The smell of hot dogs, doughnuts and candyfloss hung on the air. A vegetarian stall competed with the junk food, providing rice salads and quiche. Sara saw Wayne leading Bunter on a slow plod with a small boy, Martin Pearson, clinging to his back.

'Hold him on,' she called out as the child slipped

sideways. Wayne grinned cheerfully and grabbed a handful of red T-shirt.

The vicar, Arnold Butler, came to her side, chuckling at the sight.

'Enjoying yourself?' He eyed her with avuncular interest. 'I saw George yesterday. He's worried you're taking too much on your shoulders.'

'I'm fine. Who could be anything else on such a wonderful day?'

He nodded. The fête, set in a carpet of green with a blue sky above and a pleasant breeze, provided all the ingredients for a perfect spring day. Dressed in a cool white sundress with a blazer in pale pastel stripes and a boater perched on her head, Sara looked young and carefree.

'I hear Callum Grant is giving you some help. That's kind of him.'

'Cal's been very helpful.' She kept her voice even. Narrowing her eyes against the sun's glare, she caught sight of the man in question.

'I see you're getting the roof done; that must be a relief. I know the damp in some of the upper rooms worried George.'

'Yes. Cal had the wonderful idea of using St Clair's as a conference centre. We'll need all the rooms in good repair.'

It was like playing chess, she reflected, the curiosity generated about Callum Grant's visits to St Clair's growing daily. Cal came into sight, holding Martin Pearson's hand.

'Did you see where he came from? Someone should tell Wayne to bring the little kids back.'

'Hello, Martin.' Sara crouched beside the child,

taking her handkerchief and mopping his face. He knew her and stopped crying. 'Where's Mummy?'

'Mrs Pearson,' the vicar called, and beckoned.

A woman came over, looking agitated. She had a toddler in tow and a pushchair with a huge bag weighing down one side.

'Oh, thank goodness! I thought I'd lost him. Thank you, Sara.' She cast a quick glance at Cal. Wendy Pearson worked in the tea-shop. The trauma of Martin's disappearance over with, she was as curious as the rest.

'Actually, Mr—Cal——' Sara felt his gaze upon her '—found him. I'll just go and have a word with Wayne.'

She left Cal being effusively thanked and, she guessed, about to endure a similar interrogation from the vicar.

Later, she was judging the show-jumping under-elevens class when Callum Grant joined her.

'Did you enter this kind of thing when you were their age?' he enquired, watching the earnest young faces.

'Yes.' She searched for criticism but he merely raised an eyebrow and she looked away.

'How about now?'

Her attention was ostensibly given to the next contestant. 'I ride for pleasure. I haven't time to pursue it seriously.'

'You could have been a model without much effort.' He smiled as her lips formed a silent 'ooh'. 'You don't want to be a champion show-jumper or a model. What did you dream about, Sara? There must have been something. You can't have been married to St Clair's all your life.'

'I think there was a time when I wanted to be a vet,' she offered lightly. 'Too much James Herriot, I suspect. What about you?' she tossed the ball back into his court.

He winced in sympathy as a red-faced young hopeful slid over the neck of her piebald pony.

'Deep-sea diver. Too much Jacques Cousteau.' He made her smile. 'I did it for a while. Worked for some crazy archaeologist chasing Spanish gold.'

'Did you find any?'

'Sure. He spent all his on another project that proved fruitless. I bought into a failing business that needed investment and new management. I still back him sometimes. I like to gamble and, even if it doesn't pay off, some of the stuff he brings back is interesting.'

Callum Grant sounded as if he'd had a colourful past. Her curiosity was teased. She had been on the usual skiing holidays and around Europe's cities to visit the art museums. She had studied fine art and music at university. Her travels had left little to chance. She had stayed with family friends and studied rather than search out the street-life of anywhere she had visited. Sara began to wonder if she had played too safe. Nothing had equipped her to deal with a man like Callum Grant.

The rosettes duly distributed, she strolled with the American back towards the house. 'Do you want to go in? I've got something to do.'

'What?' He was wearing an off-white suit and black T-shirt. His jacket was slung over his shoulder.

'Er——' she tried to avoid his gaze '—just—it won't take a minute.'

'What won't?' He smiled at her embarrassment and she coloured a rosy pink.

'The maze,' she admitted. 'I usually check it. Young couples find it very alluring.'

'So?' He seemed to find the idea perfectly understandable.

'The security guard exercises his dog in there. That wouldn't be quite so romantic. It's a vicious brute.'

'OK, I'll come with you.' Sliding his arm around her shoulders, he slowed her down to a saunter. 'Why rush? It's a nice evening.'

It was a nice evening but Sara would have preferred to walk ten miles in a blizzard than be in the maze, alone, with Callum Grant.

'No one's here,' he observed, tilting his head to study her profile. 'Maybe romance has gone out of mazes. Seems a shame, I think it's romantic.' He turned her into his arms, looking past her at the golden blur of a sunset. 'Why the panic?' His sudden attention made her tense. 'You've kissed me before.'

'*I* didn't kiss *you*,' she corrected him, standing stiffly in the circle of his arms.

'It's a fine distinction.' His eyes flickered from her eyes to her mouth. The scent from the yew hedge and the sound of swifts wheeling overhead provided an evocative atmosphere. Carelessly, he threw his jacket on to the ground. Her straw boater followed. Surveying her hunted expression, he took hold of the lapels of her jacket.

'Do you know what I think? Don't hide.' He gathered her hair up, holding it, tilting her head back. 'I think things been quiet around you for too long.'

Something of his meaning impressed Sara. She could

imagine him, his hair wet, the sun on his back, sitting on a boat. Her eyes had a dreamy quality, riveting the male watching her. Her lashes closed as his mouth brushed hers.

It was dangerous to fall under the spell of his sexual magnetism. Protest hammered in her brain but reluctant envy of those young couples, not much younger than she, tempted her to sample the heady feeling of sexual pleasure. That he could provide all she needed, she didn't doubt. Just kissing her, he set her blood alight. His fingers traced her ear and she shivered as he eased back the collar of her jacket and kissed the join of her neck.

'Cal——' She broke into speech, feeling vulnerable and emotionally disturbed. Letting her lips brush his hair and her nostrils breathe in his scent rather contradicted her protest.

'Far too quiet,' he summed up, easing back, regarding the smoky blue of her eyes and the soft curve of her lips with regret. 'Did I tell you the vicar warned me off?' He bent to pick up his jacket and collected the straw hat, placing it on her head at a jaunty angle.

'What?' She accepted his arm around her shoulders without thought.

'I reassured him that my intentions were honourable. I get the impression that if I don't treat you right, I'm going to be run out of town.'

'Oh.' She was touched by the concern shown, but at the same time something inside her rebelled against the confines of safety.

They strolled around the house, passing by the cars of the stall-holders, the last to go home.

'Well, they all know now,' he murmured as the interested faces noted their intimacy.

'Yes.' She shrugged his arm away and walked ahead of him. He didn't follow her. She was rather surprised at that. 'Of course,' she muttered to herself. 'Purpose served. On to the next item of business.'

Why that annoyed her, she didn't ponder.

CHAPTER THREE

SARA took the tour scheduled for eleven o'clock. She regularly did that particular session. It was one of the busiest and they catered mainly for foreign parties. Sara could speak French and Italian fluently and could hobble by in German so she was the obvious choice. That particular day, the party were mostly Japanese with a smattering of Americans.

Dressed in a soft wool jumper in honey and cream, with a cream linen skirt, she was the very essence of casual elegance. Her outfit was complimented and gave her the opportunity to reveal that the jumper was an example of the knitwear available in the souvenir shop.

Upon request Sara dutifully posed near the Adam fireplace as the tourists added to their holiday snaps. She had been up since six, checking the deliveries from the bakery and butchers and making sure the menu for the tea-shop and more prestigious restaurant were as varied as possible. David Bresslaw came into sight and, slightly behind him, her soon-to-be husband.

'How long has the house been in the family?' an elderly woman asked. It was all in the brochure but Sara answered politely.

'Three hundred years. Not direct descent, of course, various offshoots of the family have possessed it at different times.'

'That's a long time,' someone else murmured.

'Yes.' She smiled briefly, conscious of the man

observing her. Callum Grant was dressed in a grey suit with a maroon silk tie. He didn't look uncomfortable in suits, she decided, it was just his physical vitality that confounded the well-groomed image. He gestured for her to carry on and she gathered her scattered wits with difficulty, directing her party to the cabinets containing delicate porcelain that her great-grandmother had collected.

Several times on the tour she caught a glimpse of Cal or their paths crossed, but it wasn't until she visited the restaurant that he bade her join his table. David Bresslaw was with him. The young man appeared flattered by the invitation to break bread with the great man, Sara rather less delighted by the prospect.

'You work long hours, honey.' Cal poured her a glass of wine, a knowing glint in his eyes as his expressed opinion of her lifestyle hung between them.

'We girls have to do something while we wait for Mr Right.' She picked up the wine glass, annoyed when he continued to study her with a lazy regard.

'You're not a women's libber, then?' David Bresslaw interjected, somewhat conscious of his employer's silence.

'I rather dislike labels.' She smiled coolly. 'They can be misleading.'

Callum Grant released her from his gaze, turning his attention to the people in the restaurant. If he recognised the reproof for his assumptions about her lifestyle, he showed no sign of the barb going home.

'You only run this when the house is open.' It was a statement rather than a question. 'Why's that?'

She blinked and then realised it had never occurred

to her to do otherwise. 'It's always been done that way.'

'Not any more. Besides Ravenswood, there's nothing comparable in the surrounding villages. I'll have it checked out.'

She shrugged, her mouth set mutinously.

'Don't you like the idea, Sara?' He pinned her with his gaze.

'I didn't say that.' She avoided confrontation, knowing that the restaurant trade didn't depend on the house being open. Those dining didn't often bother with the tour, merely walked in the grounds or just came for a good-quality meal.

'Worried about the workload?' he pursued her relentlessly.

'No.' She seethed inwardly. She would have welcomed the idea put by someone else and was annoyed she hadn't thought about it.

'I expect change is a little difficult to handle when you have a lot on your mind,' David Bresslaw helped her out. 'How is your father, Sara?'

'Improving.' She smiled at him more warmly. 'Thank you for asking.'

'You look tired,' the American commented. 'Are you eating properly?'

'Yes, thank you.' She was icily polite.

He didn't mention it further, but she received the distinct impression that the subject wasn't closed. Later that evening Mrs Pagett came in with a tray, looking rather apologetic. On it was a sandwich and a glass of milk. Sara was busily hand-painting one of the miniature models of St Clair's they sold to tourists.

'Thanks.' She wiped her hands on her stained dungarees, a sheaf of blonde hair swept back impatiently with her fingers. 'I am rather hungry.'

'Mr Grant thought you might be,' the housekeeper intimated. She was clearly curious as to the American's right to give orders at St Clair's.

'Is Cal still here?' She bit into a sandwich and with a sinking heart saw Mrs Pagett nod.

'He's in your father's study.'

'I see.' She lifted her shoulders, trying to ease the ache there. 'Mr Grant is helping get St Clair's organised as a proper business proposition. Both he and Mr Bresslaw will be here rather a lot over the next few weeks. Will you see they get everything they want?'

'Certainly, miss.' Mrs Pagett viewed Sara St Clair with a knowing air. 'It's nice of him to help you.'

'Mmm, isn't it?' An imp of mischief shone in her eyes. She was rather amused by how many people attributed the word 'nice' or 'kind' to Callum Grant's supposed benevolence.

Mrs Pagett looked embarrassed. 'I wasn't being inquisitive, miss. I think you could do with some help. It's a big responsibility, a house like this, and you work so very hard.'

'We all do.' Sara's voice was warm. 'Don't worry, we'll muddle through. I'm sure Cal will have us back in the black within the month.'

'A year, maybe,' a voice interrupted from the doorway. 'Eat.' He pointed at the sandwich, coming into the workshop and inspecting her handiwork. He was still in his suit but the tie had been pulled away from the collar and the top button opened. Mrs Pagett withdrew discreetly. Picking up one of the replicas, he studied it critically.

'Don't tell me,' she said. 'You're going to bring in a machine to knock out hundreds.'

'Not at all,' he answered her with mock-seriousness. 'Craftwork is big business.' He continued to explore while she finished eating. 'What are you going to tell your father, Sara?' he asked when she had finished the milk and put the glass back on the tray.

'I'll show him the plans and say that you want to pay some kind of fee to use St Clair's for business conferences. Perhaps you could have something of the sort drafted. That will ease his mind for now.'

'Not bad,' he acknowledged with a nod of approval. 'I'll see to it. Do you want me to speak to him——?' His eyes narrowed as she shook her head.

'I'd rather you kept away from my father.'

'And why is that?' He closed the distance between them and she shifted nervously on her stool, wanting to get up and run away.

'It's between us, isn't it?' Her delicate skin coloured as he lifted her chin.

'Yes, it's between us,' he agreed silkily. 'Take those dungarees off. I don't want paint all over me.'

'I——' She swallowed drily. 'I will not!'

'Why?' His intent appraisal noted the cotton shirt she had underneath. 'Does that belong to an old boyfriend?'

'No, my grandfather.' She felt her body bathed in a similar heat to her face.

'So what's the problem?' He undid the clasp on one strap of her dungarees and it fell down to her waist. Slowly, with his eyes on hers, he eased the other one off her shoulder. Noting her embarrassment, he took her face between his hands, kissing her deeply and without preliminaries. Sara shook with conflicting desires that made her want to slap his face and move closer into his embrace at the same time.

He pulled her up against him. The dungarees slithered to her feet. She was wearing nothing in the way of stockings, and when she stepped out of them her bare legs encountered the cool material of his suit, the shirt covering her upper thighs providing flimsy protection. His fingers caressed her nape and she tilted her head back at the agony and ecstasy felt in her cramped muscles. Sensing her need, he massaged her shoulders, the gaping neckline of the collarless shirt falling apart as he magically dispensed with the buttons, so that it rested, stretched over her upper arms, drawn tight across the swell of her breasts. Pressing kisses just below her ear and along the line of her jaw, his mouth found hers again, his hands warm on her neck, his thumbs moving against the small bones at the base of her throat.

Sinking fast, Sara tried to keep her anger alive. She escaped his marauding mouth only to have her lips slide over the roughness of his jaw and linger there. His skin was tanned and tough, the alien beauty of his bone-structure a relentless denial of anything soft or gentle. The sheer potency of his masculinity stunned her. Somewhere in the twilight of her subconscious, Sara knew a wondrous feeling of discovery.

Framing her face with his hands, Callum Grant appraised the confusion in Sara's eyes. It was fascinating to him the way she could be spitting fury at him one moment and then be innocent and intensely vulnerable the next. In some ways he was as far out of his depth as she was.

Disturbed by the thought, he provoked her rather than fall to the temptation of her naked shoulders and half-bared breasts. His fingers resting lightly on her shoulders, his gaze wandered over her state of dishabille.

'Beautiful but cold, that's what the guys in your set say about you. I've never had a woman with a reputation like that. No—that's wrong.' He was infuriatingly insolent. 'You don't have a reputation.'

'And you haven't had me!' Her blue eyes were proud, the drowsiness of passion disappearing fast. Pulling the shirt back into place, she turned away.

'Not yet. But I will,' he said quietly, sending a shiver down her spine.

Bridling at his tone, she was unknowingly provocative, the man's shirt ridiculously large. 'It gives you pleasure, does it? Buying what otherwise you wouldn't stand a chance of attaining.'

His smile admired and mocked at the same time. 'I'm saving you from a barren obsession with a pile of bricks. Get some sleep,' he advised dismissively. The 'You'll need it,' that followed was meant to inflame her and was entirely successful.

'You specialise in vulgarity,' she accused him, her voice coated in ice.

He raised an eyebrow. 'The place needs a lot doing to it. What are you talking about?' The innocence was even passably performed.

Sara had forcibly to stop herself lashing out at him, and the effort made her shake. She had never met such a maddening man—and to think she had let him kiss her like that! The thought was unbearable. So was the fact that her body was still suffering from pangs of withdrawal.

'Goodnight, Sara.' The slow once-over he gave her showed how little her anger or her feelings moved him.

'If you say "sweet dreams" I won't be responsible,' she muttered between clenched teeth.

'I don't think you'll find it easy to sleep.' He winked at her and left the room.

Collapsing on to the stool, she rested her arms against her workbench and buried her face against them. The silence in the room wasn't the peaceful balm she expected. Adrenalin raged through her blood and a new, unexpectedly powerful feeling of frustration made her skin hot and uncomfortable.

One of her former suitors, Gareth Haldane, had buried himself in the wilds of Peru to forget her and she had thought the gesture rather ridiculous. She began to have some sympathy for his plight. Peru seemed preferable to becoming Callum Grant's plaything, especially when she suspected he could make her enjoy the humiliation.

'Are you all right, miss?' Mrs Pagett asked, sounding rather embarrassed.

'What——?' She lifted her head and spotted the dungarees between them in a crumpled heap on the floor. The draught from the door cooled her bare legs.

'Oh—yes, I—er—spilt paint.' She could feel the hot tide of colour begin at her toes and advance rapidly towards her neck and face. 'I'll clean up the mess, don't worry.'

Mrs Pagett nodded, her neat figure very proper

except for a slight failure to meet Sara's eyes. Callum Grant, Sara reflected, was going to shake up St Clair's and all in it. Suddenly an image of Mrs Pagett bringing in tea while Cal's body tangled with hers in a sea of crisp white cotton leapt to mind, and she pressed her hands against the twin flags of colour staining her cheeks. Such images tormented her dreams, and when she got up the next morning she hardly felt rested at all. Sweet dreams, she suspected, were things of the past.

Sara was surprised to see June Douglas, her assistant, in early the next morning. She was usually on her own when the first of the daily provisions arrived.

'I'll count the bread rolls if you like,' the woman volunteered. She was in her mid-thirties, dark-haired, very jolly and sometimes rather blunt.

'Thank you.' Sara observed her discreetly. They worked in close harmony, checking through the order books. The bakers usually delivered first, then the butchers. The vegetables came from the market and arrived around ten o'clock when the kitchen staff were there to note any shortfall or deterioration in quality.

'Tea?' June put on the kettle as Sara nodded and they had a break before the arrival of the butcher's van from March Haverling.

'Sara?' June began as they sat down at the long table used to prepare the food. Around them huge copper saucepans hung on hooks and rows of sharp knives gleamed.

'Yes?' The fair woman sipped her tea, expecting a heart-to-heart. June Douglas mediated between the St

Clairs and the staff, and Sara guessed some issue had brought her in that morning.

'Well, you know I'm hopeless at being subtle so I'll get straight to the point. Are we going to become part of Callum Grant's business empire or what? It's causing a good deal of gossip, his auditor being here, and I think—no, I know the staff are worried about losing their jobs.'

'Yes, I'm sorry, they must be.' She had been so absorbed in her father's plight and the intrusion of Callum Grant in her life, she had forgotten that the stately home was one of the largest employers in the immediate district. 'No one need worry about a take-over. St Clair's will stay under my father's control. Callum Grant's company means to use St Clair's as a conference centre. The repairs are part of a deal negotiated between Cal and myself.' The fiction tripped off her tongue with ease. Before long, she reflected sardonically, she'd begin to believe it herself. 'As far as employment is concerned, we shall possibly be expanding rather than the reverse. I'm sorry if I've been uncommunicative.' She smiled apologetically. 'I've had a lot on my mind.'

June Douglas chuckled. 'Not least of which is Callum Grant himself. Quite a man.'

Shrugging modestly, Sara realised that most people thought she was fortunate to have Cal for an admirer.

'I hear Gareth Haldane will be home shortly. He won't be very happy to find our American friend in residence.'

'He isn't in residence, and Gareth and I are just friends.' Unlike many women, Sara liked to keep her private life exactly that. Gareth Haldane's return from

Peru pleased her, as would the return of any friend, but it went no deeper than that. The Haldane estate was large and had, over the years, acquired much of the farmland belonging to St Clair's. A romantic attachment between Sara and Gareth had been predicted from the cradle, the convenience of it making many of their acquaintances see it as almost inevitable. Sara herself was the fly in the ointment. She was glad she'd had the sense to resist the pleasant, attractive man Gareth Haldane undoubtedly was. He had never kept her awake with dreams so powerful that they still lingered in her mind in the light of day. She detested Callum Grant, but he had taught her, in a few short lessons, that she had a passionate nature. Such a nature, unfulfilled, would provide a catastrophic basis for marriage.

'Mrs Pagett thinks you're in terrible danger of being compromised.' June Douglas winked, unabashed.

'I think Mrs Pagett is a little old-fashioned,' Sara remarked non-committally. 'That sounds like the butcher. Shall we get on?'

'You're no fun, Sara,' the older woman complained good-humouredly.

'Nonsense.' She grinned. 'It's much more intriguing to be mysterious.' That tickled June Douglas's sense of humour.

'Hmm, well, watch out. Gareth may be a lamb, but Callum Grant is a big bad wolf if ever I saw one, and he's definitely on the prowl.'

The subject of Callum Grant's involvement with St Clair's came up again when her father became worried about the cost of a private room. Sara was on her daily visit when he asked about how they could possibly afford the bill.

'We've been rather lucky, Daddy.' She hated the deception and it took a great deal of effort to keep her tone light. 'Callum Grant wants to use St Clair's for business meetings. You know how Americans are about the old country. He's being very generous.'

'Oh, yes?' He regarded her steadily, bushy eyebrows lowered, searching her features. He looked worried. Being left with a daughter on the brink of adolescence wasn't easy for a man. He'd left Sara's 'life education' in the hands of the boarding-school and hadn't been displeased with the result. Not until, that was, Gareth Haldane's besotted admiration had been barely perceived by his daughter. If she had a similar blind spot about Grant, he feared for the consequences.

'Sara. Do you like Callum Grant? I mean he's not— well, you're not used to that sort of man.'

'Cal's certainly different,' she agreed, trying to sound starry-eyed. Dressed in white cotton trousers and a pillarbox-red sweatshirt, her fair hair tied back in a pony-tail, she looked young and brimming with enthusiasm. 'He's got the whole thing planned out so the necessary alterations will cause the minimum disruption. He also thinks it might help if we opened the restaurant out of season.'

George St Clair leant back against the pillows, closing his eyes. 'I don't see Grant as anyone's Good Fairy. Watch your step, darling.'

'I will.' She kissed his forehead. 'Cal isn't an ogre, Daddy. He's just had to fight hard for what he's got. I admire him for that.'

'Yes.' He nodded but still looked perturbed. Having

his daughter pursued by a man he had heard one appreciative young woman call 'a stud' made him feel uncomfortable. Most of his acquaintances praised him for what they called Sara's good old-fashioned standards. He had never pried into her personal life, but, if she was inexperienced with men, taking on the American struck him as dangerously ambitious.

'Men like Grant don't like being teased, Sara, and you can be flirtatious. I don't think you do it on purpose,' he stumbled on desperately. 'But you're a beautiful woman. And——' He took a steadying breath, trying to put it tactfully. 'I don't think you realise how susceptible men are to female beauty.'

Sara smiled mischievously. 'I'll come again tomorrow. Don't worry, Cal and I—well, we don't play those sort of games.'

The performance left her drained. A limousine drew up beside her as she left the hospital. Glancing sideways, she ignored it and went to her own car.

Stephen Appleton waved to her facetiously and she matched the gesture, pulling out of the car park and driving totally without direction. The need to get away was strong. She had to visit the hospital the next day but, apart from a short phone call to Mrs Pagett to tell her she wouldn't be home, she declared the day her own.

After driving for a while, she drew into the drive of the Limes. Angela Carter lived there with her brother Daniel. Daniel was an artist and Angela ran the gallery in March Haverling where he exhibited his paintings.

'I hope you're not expecting dinner,' Daniel greeted her. 'Angela burnt it.'

Daniel affected a Byronic image and his sister had

similar dark, good looks. Both preferred the Limes to the rather strict regime run by their father at Chatswick House.

'You were supposed to be watching the time,' Angela complained. 'I was on the phone.'

'You're never off the phone.' He gave Sara a rather generous gin and tonic. 'There you are, love, you look as if you need it.'

'Thanks.' She smiled at her friends and walked through the french windows, out on to the patio. They followed her, each taking one of the cushioned garden chairs. It was another lovely evening, the sky aflame with red and gold. Informality was the keynote at the Limes, and Sara treated it very much as a home from home.

'I think it's a case of "if you can't run, hide",' Angela observed sweetly. 'Has that gorgeous hunk been chasing you around St Clair's? He's never out of the place by all accounts.'

'Not that we ever listen to gossip,' Daniel interjected with mock pomposity. 'Angela, leave the girl alone. She will tell us if she wants to. Until then, we will help her through her time of trial.'

'Idiot.' Sara couldn't help laughing. 'I just need a change of scenery. Can I stay tonight?'

'Of course you can.' Angela kept her tone light, giving her brother a meaningful look. He nodded. Sara St Clair didn't often ask for help, however obliquely. She looked bone-weary and they kept the conversation casual, pretending not to notice when she drifted off into a world of her own.

Sara was reliving Callum's kisses the evening before, trying to understand what was happening to her. She should be glad to be out of his way for the evening but, even with the companionship of her old friends, she felt flat in mood. Perhaps it was the strain of the last few weeks catching up with her.

Callum Grant was an attractive male, she tried to put her response into context. He was an experienced lover and at least ten years her senior. She was only human! The knowledge did little to cool the fire in her blood. He was careful with her though, the thought suddenly popped into her head. Now why should she think that?

'Cocoa, Sara?' Daniel joked.

She frowned non-comprehendingly, the blaze of blue between her dark lashes making him swallow drily.

'Little Sara's growing up,' he commented to his sister when their guest had gone to bed.

'Poor Gareth,' she sympathised with their absent friend.

'Mmm.' Daniel was non-committal. 'Grant's a tough customer. Sara won't escape him easily if he wants to keep her.'

'Why would she want to?' Angela rather envied her friend.

'Gareth's more your cup of tea. You could boss him mercilessly.'

Daniel Carter got a wet dishcloth around his ear for his observations.

Headlights momentarily lit up the kitchen and Angela peered out. Stephen Appleton got out of his car and walked over to where Sara's was parked. Daniel craned his neck to see what his sister was looking at.

'Do you think Stephen's turned car thief to boost his income?' Daniel Carter's voice was whimsical.

'Vintage Morris Oxfords aren't easy to move.' His sister affected the accent of a Chicago ganster. 'I'd say he was checking up. And we know who for, don't we?'

Sara had also been attracted to the bedroom window by the car's lights. She watched Stephen Appleton return to his own vehicle and turned away from the window. Getting back into bed, she shivered, her flesh goose-pimpling. What had she got herself into?

CHAPTER FOUR

SARA was furious the next day to find Callum Grant speaking to her father. His disruptive presence in the quiet sanctum of the hospital was something she hadn't been prepared to deal with. It was like letting a jungle beast into an art gallery, she thought, contrasting Cal with the more civilised aspects of her life.

'Oh.' She quickly covered up her feelings. 'Cal. I didn't expect to see you here.' Conscious of her parent's interest, she tried to look pleased.

Fortunately, her father's attention remained on her. Cal's intent appraisal went beyond the bounds of decency. Looking extremely male in casual well-worn denim, he raked back his hair with his fingers as if the sight of her made him hot. 'You weren't at the house.' Their eyes tangled, each maintaining a pleasant front.

'I'm never very hard to find.' Her chin lifted challengingly, the memory of Stephen Appleton's bloodhound activities firing her anger. 'What did you want?'

A reluctant smile included her father into their circle. 'That's the last question a pretty girl should ask a man. Haven't you told her that, George?'

George St Clair chuckled. Sara's smile was manufactured. That easy male charm didn't fool her for a minute. Her bid for freedom had not been appreciated. If she did something he didn't like, he would reciprocate fully. The message was very clear.

'I thought we'd agreed you would stay away from Daddy,' she hissed as soon as they were out of earshot.

He shrugged negligently. 'It's his house, at least for the moment. It would look odd if I didn't consult him. Don't worry.' He was dry. 'I didn't mess things up for you. I can be diplomatic.'

'I'm sure.' Tossing her hair back, she quickened her pace intending to leave him in her wake.

'Sara——' His voice never rose above a quiet purr but it stopped her dead in her tracks.

Resentful, and feeling like a bad-mannered child, she waited for him, sending him a barely conciliatory glance as he put his arm around her shoulders.

'That isn't necessary,' she said as she felt his fingers tighten.

'I like to feel your body close to mine.' The muted aggression in his steady regard contradicted his expressed desire. 'Besides, I believe the couple in the Porsche are friends of yours.'

Sara conceded the truth of the statement with a sinking heart. It was the Cairnses, and they were taking in the close proximity of Callum Grant and Sara with interest.

'This is all so detestable,' she muttered as they moved towards Cal's car, meeting the couple as they crossed the car park.

'Hello,' Margaret Cairns greeted Sara warmly. 'Cal.' Her bright eyes moved from one to the other. 'We thought we'd pop in on George, but if you think it would tire him we'll leave it for now.'

'He's had a busy morning.' Cal was firm. 'Maybe later in the evening he would appreciate the company. Sara and I have a previous engagement.'

It was the first Sara had heard of it but she gritted her teeth and managed the usual pleasantries.

'I object to the way you take over my life,' she informed him glacially as he slid into the car beside her.

'Tough.' Cal started up the engine, ignoring her surprised expression, and flicked on a cassette.

He was annoyed, Sara realised, taking a furtive glance at his profile. Her disappearance had got under his skin. What did he expect, she continued a silent argument—for her to give up her independence and become a total doormat for him to wipe his feet on?

She watched, unwillingly fascinated as he drove with the confident assertiveness that marked everything he did. There was a brooding quality to his features; despite his apparent concentration on the road, his mind was elsewhere. His long brown fingers spun the wheel as he negotiated a tight bend and the alien quality about him had never seemed stronger to Sara.

'Where are we going?' She sounded subdued and he spared her a glance.

'London. Your housekeeper packed some things for you. We'll stay over. Tomorrow, we'll go shopping. You need some clothes.'

He really was the most high-handed man! 'When you say we'll stay——'

'I mean we'll stay at my apartment in Knightsbridge. Do you object?' The mockery was unsheathed.

'Would it make a difference?' Sara was beginning to feel exhausted by the struggle. It was an unfair battle. Her only escape was to wound her father, and she loved him too much for that.

'No,' he said bluntly. 'Don't you enjoy having money spent on you? Most women do.'

Sara gave him a cold look and turned her head away to look out of the side window.

'Look at it as a business expense. My associates expect me to keep a beautiful, well-groomed wife.'

Sara closed her eyes, cooling her temple against the glass. 'I'm surprised you want me,' she said quietly, sounding as dispirited as she felt.

His laughter was low and derisory. 'I'm not in a complimentary mood.'

She digested this, sinking even further into her seat. 'I wasn't fishing for compliments. I just find your obsessional interest something of a mystery.'

If he had been in a better mood, she received the impression he would have laughed; instead a smile curled his lips. 'Not much of a mystery—you don't have my hormones!'

She was glad of the gloom of the grey skies to hide her sudden agitation. 'You wouldn't consider marriage because of that.' She sounded harassed. 'I mean, I'm sure there have been plenty of occasions when——' Expression failed her.

'My hormones went crazy?' His mood seemed to lighten. 'I'm thirty-six—what do you think?'

'Well, then?'

'I told you. I want a wife. You're my fairy princess in a beautiful castle.'

'Oh, yes?'

Her disbelief made him send her a humorous glance. 'So I'm romantic—sue me.'

She bit her lip to stop smiling in response. It would

be dreadful to find any semblance of rapport with the enemy.

'This apartment—has it more than one bedroom?'

Pushing his lip out thoughtfully, he pretended to consider the matter. 'Five.'

She was annoyed that he should keep her on tenter-hooks. 'Well, I shall want one to myself, otherwise I shall spend the evening with friends.'

'We'll get married next month.' Cal changed gears with a lack of fluidity that spoke volumes.

Sara sat back, pleased with her victory. Perhaps he wasn't as formidable as she had first thought.

That Callum Grant intended to put her to work immediately became apparent when they met an older couple at the Royal Ballet performance of *Romeo and Juliet*. Cal disappeared with Sir Victor Johnson, a gruff Northerner who had earned his knighthood for his business endeavours.

Helen Johnson inclined her head towards the closing door of the box. 'Get used to that, my dear, Victor and Cal are cut from the same cloth.'

So it seemed. Sara, although not desiring his company, found his sudden lack of interest insulting. He had almost kidnapped her, not for the purpose of furthering their intimacy as she had feared but so that she could keep Sir Victor's wife company while they talked business.

The two men joined them in the interval. Cal talked generally about the States as they sipped chilled white wine, responding to Helen Johnson's interest. While he spoke his fingers lightly ran back and forward over the curve of Sara's shoulder. The black velvet evening dress Mrs Pagett had packed but, she suspected, not chosen had only the thinnest of straps. His touch burnt trackways into her skin and she fought not to shiver.

'Are you going to watch the rest of the performance?' Her voice was husky and a little plaintive.

'Lonely?' He looped a stray strand of hair behind her ear, dark eyes wandering over the classical beauty of her profile and the vulnerable line of her neck. 'I like it when you wear your hair up, it suits you.'

'I think you're being rather rude,' she said quietly, the other couple distracted by the unexpected arrival of friends.

'You do?' He nodded as if he was well aware of her opinion of his manners. 'What you need, honey, is money, not an impoverished *gentleman*. Remember that.'

Picking up her drink, she tried to ignore him, but his fingers began to play with the baby hairs at her nape.

'Cal!' she protested, most uncomfortable.

His fingers stroked down to the low back of her dress. 'You're so easily shocked.' His voice sounded deep and warm next to her ear. 'I'm not keen on ballet. Another black mark, huh?'

'You don't care what I think. Why pretend that you do?' Sara's blue eyes were unknowingly vulnerable and Cal's mocking attitude changed to something more serious. He didn't say anything but, much to Sara's surprise, followed her back to the box. Sir Victor, robbed of his companion, joined them too.

They went on for supper afterwards and returned to Cal's apartment after twelve that night.

Used to the traditional décor of St Clair's, Sara found Cal's apartment modern and yet tasteful at the same time. Browns, golds and the odd splash of brilliant colour gave it a rich earthy quality. It had an ethnic feel without representing any particular culture.

There were a thousand questions she wanted to ask him. She had gleaned from listening to his conversation with Victor Johnson that his main field of interest was data communications. It had never occurred to her to ask what he did. His origins fascinated her as well. Where did that Latin colouring come from? Where had he grown up? Did he have any family? The words trembled on her lips but Cal forestalled her. Dropping a light kiss on her mouth, he pushed her gently towards her bedroom.

'You look all in. I'll make breakfast,' he promised.

Sara hesitated, turning to see him pick up his briefcase. 'I suppose you're going to work.' She didn't know why but she didn't like the idea.

'Any objections?' He gave her a quizzical look.

'Don't you ever sleep?'

'Yes, I sleep.' He pulled his tie free and undid the top two buttons of his shirt. That bold, over-familiar look was back in his eyes. 'But if you've got a problem——'

'Goodnight, Cal.' She retreated hastily, panic making her clumsy.

The last impression of him before she shut the door was of white teeth flashing in amusement and she heard him say, 'Sara, you're priceless,' before the door clicked and she was rid of his irritating presence.

Turning restlessly, Sara's lashes parted and she stared hard into the darkness. The room wasn't familiar and the raised beat of her heart increased its tempo.

Scrambling out of bed, she groped for the light switch and winced as it illuminated the room. Slowly, the lost, lonely feeling was replaced by the knowledge that she was in Cal's apartment. Instinct prompted her to find him. Why his presence should comfort her, she didn't ponder.

'Sara?' Cal came out of his study, attracted by her movements. Rubbing his chest wearily, he viewed the strappy oyster-coloured nightdress she wore with dedicated interest. 'Can't sleep?' An ironic gleam entered his eyes when he realised she was totally oblivious to his regard.

'I didn't know where I was.' She pushed a hand through her hair, blue eyes drowsy with sleep. 'I'd better ring and see how Daddy is.'

'Sara,' he clamped his hand over hers as she tried to pick up the receiver, 'it's two in the morning.'

'What? Oh, yes.' She blinked, her head clearing. 'How stupid of me.'

'You're just a little disorientated.' Putting his arm around her shoulders, he led her back to her bedroom. 'Bad dreams?' he questioned softly.

'No—I don't know.' Her eyes lifted to his, noticing the dark shadow around his jaw and the heavy cast of his tanned features. 'I suppose so.'

The bed loomed large in the room, the crumpled sheets and dizzy display of pillows telling their own story. Sara was very aware of Cal. He confused her with his hot and cold tactics; it suggested a control she didn't possess.

Silently, he moved past her and straightened the bottom sheet, gathering the pillows and replacing them. No one had performed such a task for her since she was very young.

'Are you worried about your father?' Cal let her off the hook.

She nodded, knowing her restless sleep had nothing to do with her father's illness. She was confident he was on the road to recovery. It didn't matter what social conventions he chose to preserve; the satin nightgown clearly outlined the hardened peaks of her breasts and Cal's regard became increasingly intimate.

'I'll call Steve, I asked him to check with the hospital.' He turned his back on her, the silence between them laden with unspoken desires. When he got through, he spoke quickly into the receiver and nodded when he heard the reply. 'OK. Sorry for getting you out of bed, Steve.'

'He's fine,' he said as he turned back to her. 'No problem.'

'Thank you.' She was grateful and her eyes warmed, elevating her beauty from the cool and classical to something infinitely more sensual.

Cal's gaze flicked from the satin that covered her breasts to her lips and met her eyes with a potent force that hit her like a blow.

'I think left to yourself you'd be too proud to come to any man.' He brushed her lips with the back of his thumb. 'Which would be a shame.' He drew the covers away from her body. 'Because I have the feeling that you've got a lot to offer.'

Sara felt hurt, her blue eyes large in her face. 'I don't know why you provoke me,' she accused him huskily. 'It's almost as if you want us to fight.'

'I don't want to fight,' he denied, bending his head

to kiss her shoulder. Looking up, his eyes were molten. 'I want to see how you look when my fingers have been through your hair and I've kissed your mouth until it becomes soft and sweet under mine.'

Sara swallowed drily. He leant over her, lean and powerful, his mouth seeking hers. She knew she should resist but the words didn't reach her lips. Made vulnerable by the strangeness of her surroundings and a host of responsibilities that filled her waking hours, Sara was greatly in need of human warmth. Everyone was always so sure she could cope, it never occurred to them that there were many occasions when she longed for a shoulder to cry on. Any support Cal offered would be given at a price. He was honest about that. His lips brushed hers, dark eyes shaded by thick black lashes, taking in the tremulous movement of her mouth. Again his head bent. She could hardly bear the tension.

Her breasts strained against the oyster silk, her mouth begging for the fleeting contact to be maintained. When he retreated once more, she gazed up at him in aching torment, resistance gone, burnt away like mist under a desert sun.

The lamp illuminated the hard masculine planes of his face. Cal's gaze was steady, absorbing every shade and nuance of her expression. His own hunger made his features immobile. Unknown to Sara, Cal sensed the emotional hiatus within her and became defensive in turn. He wanted her pedigree, her style and most of all her beauty. That was the deal. He didn't want to see the shadow of inner loneliness, the tears behind the bravery. It echoed things in him that he had put down to morbid sentimentality long ago. When he finally took her mouth, it was to bury what he had uncovered. His gentleness he didn't question. Nor the fact that he was the one maintaining strict control.

Cal took it slowly. Talking softly to her between kisses, he soothed her, his tone mesmeric. Stroking his fingertips over her high cheekbones, he obeyed indulgently as she presented every part of her face for his mouth to touch. Long, drugging kisses clouded Sara's mind. Her senses were aroused unbearably. She craved this dark excitement with a hunger that sprang from the very depths of her being. It almost hurt when he touched her. She wanted to feel those strong brown fingers on every inch of her body.

Cal's dark features and the contrasting brilliant white of his dress shirt were brief impressions. His scent and aftershave tingled in her nostrils and it was a relief to give up her passivity and slide her hands under his arms and seek the strong planes of his back.

'Open my shirt,' he breathed against her mouth. 'Touch my skin.'

Sara felt his body lift so that she could obey, but his mouth kept up an assault on her senses. Blindly, she released the buttons, her hands greedy as they massaged the tight muscles of his back and her fingers followed the indentation of his spine, the damp weight of his shirt brushing her skin. Hot needles of passion burnt through her blood. She was almost mindless with the shock of it. Her mouth ached from his possession, the heated thrust of his tongue between her lips causing a sob of passionate need to communicate her feelings.

The pressure on her mouth eased and she felt his fingers spreading the gold of her hair across the pale pillowcase. Kissing her eyelids shut, he moved his lips to her ear.

'If I make a deal I stick to it.' His voice sounded unbelievably controlled. 'Do you know what you're getting yourself into, sweetheart?'

Sara suddenly focused on his face, seeing the analytical look she was being subjected to. His hand deliberately moved over the satin triangle covering her breast and palmed her flesh, his eyes steady on hers.

'You're arousing me and I don't enjoy being teased. It doesn't make sleeping very easy.' He let his eyes wander over the bed meaningfully.

Sara found it harder to surface from the passion they had shared. Somewhere a dim perception grew that Cal found it easier to buy than be given something, and that it made him wary.

'I want to see you without this.' His fingers pushed under the satin and she flinched as if his touch seared her. His crude approach was supposed to put her off but the move backfired. When he touched her he didn't want to stop, and his expression changed as he felt the stiff point of her nipple against the pad of his finger.

'Cal?' a woman's voice called, and he stiffened with an incredulous groan of pure frustration.

'I don't believe this.' Standing up, he pulled the covers over Sara and moved quickly to the door.

Before he could reach it, an elderly woman opened the door, her greeting on seeing Callum Grant warm and enthusiastic.

'Teresa.' To his credit, he tried to ease her out of the room before she noticed he had a guest. A rush of what Sara recognised to be Spanish greeted the sight of the young woman in the bed. Sara felt horribly embarrassed.

'Teresa,' he interrupted authoritatively, 'Sara and I are engaged. We're going to be married next month. Now, if you don't mind, I guess she'd like some sleep.' Dark eyes flicked back to the girl in the bed, the faint question in their depths intended to remind her how close she had been to total surrender.

'My grandmother,' he offered by way of introduction. 'She's the guardian of my virtue.'

A deep, affectionate laugh greeted the scathing response. 'I would never take on a job and do it so badly.' She spoke in English for the benefit of the Englishwoman. Noting the blush staining the girl's cheek, she relented slightly. 'Well, at least she can blush. That's an improvement on——'

'Teresa!' Cal ushered her out of the room, saying 'Goodnight,' his eyes holding an intimacy which didn't help to cool the clamour of Sara's blood.

Sara closed her eyes to shut out the world, rather than invite sleep. It seemed incredible to her that she had lived for twenty-three years without knowing she possessed such hunger. This was what it must have been like for Gareth, she reflected, and she had basked in the tenderness he offered, giving only fond affection in return. She turned restlessly, trying to find a cool place on the sheet. It seemed hours before she slept.

'Good morning.' Teresa Cortez brought in Sara's breakfast, opening the curtains and watching the girl's lashes part. 'Maybe I should have left you longer,' she commented, observing the dark shadows under Sara's eyes. 'It seems to me that you haven't been getting much sleep lately.'

'Good morning.' Sara returned the older woman's scrutiny. Teresa Cortez was silver-haired, on the plump side, and had clearly handed on qualities of stubbornness and strength to her grandson.

Sara pulled herself up into a sitting position, combing her hair with her fingers. 'That wasn't necessary.' She viewed the breakfast tray dubiously. 'You should have called me.'

'I did. You were fast asleep. Besides, I want to talk.' Teresa Cortez didn't beat around the bush. 'Are you pregnant?'

Sara's eyes widened with disbelief. 'No, I'm not! How dare——?'

'I dare.' The woman grinned at her. 'Don't get on your high horse with me, I'm an old woman and I find being subtle wastes time. So, I'm curious. How did you manage to get my grandson to promise marriage? He has avoided it very skilfully for years.'

Sara didn't know when would be the appropriate time but she felt first thing in the morning was definitely inappropriate for this kind of conversation.

'I didn't get him to promise marriage; it was the other way around, actually.' She picked up her teacup, her blue eyes steady.

'Ah.' The woman looked her up and down. 'Well, you're very beautiful, I can see that, but then he's a handsome and wealthy man. Many beautiful women throw themselves at his feet.'

'I should imagine that's where he likes them. Will you excuse me? I'd like to get dressed.'

Teresa Cortez chuckled at that. 'I'm glad to see you

can speak for yourself. I detest women who simper. They usually turn out to be vipers or totally boring.'

It was Sara's turn to smile. She had imagined Cal alone in the world, and to find a powerful Spanish matriarch frowning on his behaviour struck her as amusing.

'So, you come from a good family and you're not pregnant. Why are you staying here alone with my grandson? The newspapers hound him; it would not be proper that it should come out that you are alone together.'

Tempted to pour coals on his head, Sara relented, knowing he could be vengeful. Instead, she let his grandmother make her own deductions.

'When Cal suggested we came to London for the evening, he didn't really discuss the finer details,' she demurred. 'I didn't feel very comfortable about staying here but he said I could have my own room.'

Memories of the night before came back to haunt her and the colour came back to her cheeks. Teresa patted her hand comfortingly.

'I see. He betrayed your trust. He can't help it,' she said, shrugging. 'He's a man. They can't be trusted with such things, especially Cal.'

Sara was slightly uncomfortable with that. 'It wasn't really his fault. I woke up and didn't know where I was. I was worried about my father. Cal brought me back in here and rang Stephen Appleton to check on his condition. It wasn't really the way it looked.'

Brown eyes twinkled out of a walnut-coloured face. 'All right,' she chuckled. 'I have already told him what I think, so we will not discuss the matter again. Get dressed when you have had your breakfast. Cal is taking us shopping. I won't trouble you with my old woman's dresses, but I would like to see what the young are wearing. Do you mind?'

'Not at all,' Sara replied. The more the merrier as far as she was concerned. The presence of his grandmother would keep Cal's liberty-taking to a minimum and, after the night before, she felt she needed protection.

CHAPTER FIVE

THEY travelled back from London to St Clair's late in the afternoon. Sara was silent during most of the journey. The sports car was only a two-seater and it had been arranged that Teresa would follow them to the house the next day in one of the company limousines.

Cal's proprietorial attitude at the fashion house had re-established hostile relations. He had allowed her to select what she wished, but taken the liberty of adding several dresses to her wardrobe with an indolent, 'Indulge me,' when she complained.

'Ah, you see Sara in that one,' Teresa had teased him.

'I think that what I imagine I'll keep to myself,' he murmured, turning his head to meet his fiancée's condemnation.

'It has no back.' She viewed the model dispassionately. 'I don't particularly enjoy the thought of parading in public in that.'

'I think Chloë looks very charming.' His voice had a silken note. The model, a South American beauty, with dark, almond-shaped eyes, flashed him a smile.

'Then perhaps you should buy it for her,' Sara muttered in an undertone.

He appeared to consider the matter and glanced at the model before subjecting Sara to a long, critical look.

'I don't think I'd like you to wear it in public, Sara, but we will dine alone and you're not turning up in paint-spattered dungarees.'

'You'd prefer me in a nightdress?' She determinedly kept her eyes averted, pretending to watch another improbable creation being modelled.

'You won't need a nightdress,' he returned smoothly. 'I'll keep you warm.'

Such skirmishes reminded her of everything she disliked about Callum Grant. He could be charming when he chose and, in intimate situations, he evoked a response in her that was as fierce as it was reluctant. The important thing to remember was that he wielded a power over her that was based on the exploitation of her weaknesses. A man capable of such opportunism was unworthy of respect.

Sara visited her father that evening, steeling herself for the inevitable questions he would want to ask. No doubt the Cairnses would have acquainted him with the current gossip, and with the arrival of Teresa Cortez, bubbling over with wedding plans, her father would have to be told of the prospective marriage as soon as the moment seemed right.

George St Clair was in high spirits, teasing her about her relationship with Cal, clearly delighted that the formidable pile of bills had been methodically dealt with.

'I think you're unusually serious about Callum Grant,' he said, inviting her confidence, and Sara felt her heart lurch. She couldn't ask for a better opening than that, but for some reason the words wouldn't come. She smiled instead.

'He's been very supportive, Daddy. I'm grateful to him, naturally.'

'Margaret seemed to think you were slightly more than friends.' He chuckled at her awkwardness.

Taking a deep breath, she took the plunge. 'Actually, Daddy, Cal has asked me to marry him. I know it's sudden,' she said quickly as she saw the surprise on his face. 'But it's what we both want.'

'Good gracious!' He stared at her as if she had two heads. 'You certainly don't beat about the bush when you've made up your mind.' He shook his head dazedly. The pale blue pyjamas he was wearing were large on his thin frame and his neck had the scrawny look that age and illness brought. His eyes looked clearer, though, Sara noticed, and despite his amazement at her news he appeared more relaxed than he had done for some time. 'I don't know, after years of barely acknowledging the advances of smitten suitors you decide to marry Callum Grant after a few weeks' acquaintance.'

'I know.' She took his hands. 'But I want to marry him, Daddy. You won't object, will you? I want you to be happy for me.'

'I am happy for you, darling. It's just that—do you really know him well enough? I know he's a handsome devil and much more powerful in many ways than the men you're used to, but his life's been very different from yours. You won't be able to behave in your usual cavalier fashion with him.'

Sara was stunned by this analysis of her behaviour.

'Cavalier?' She cleared her throat, her expression perplexed. 'I don't think——'

'Darling,' George St Clair patted her hand, 'you've

had young men chauffeuring you around the country, arranging all sorts of things to surprise and delight you. You can't imagine every woman receives the same attention, and——' he felt the onus on him as a father to be a little more frank than usual '—not every man is satisfied with glowing smiles, stunning though yours may be. Callum Grant will not be cajoled into anything that doesn't suit him, of that, I'm very sure.'

Not so easily taken in, her father, Sara acknowledged. 'I don't think I'd like a man who was so gullible,' she recovered well.

George St Clair gave her a long look and met his daughter's unfaltering gaze. 'You're sure——?'

'Yes.' She smiled with manufactured delight, which was partly composed of genuine relief, and hugged him, kissing his cheek. 'Now you're not to worry, Cal and I will make all the arrangements. His grandmother, Teresa Cortez, will be staying at St Clair's. Wedding plans will distract her from the problems with the heating.' Seeing his face, she put up her hand. 'Don't worry, Cal's having central heating put in as part of the deal. He can't have his business associates blue with cold.'

'No, I expect not.' He gave her a pleased smile. 'As long as you're not rushing into anything, Sara. I must admit, after Gareth disappeared to Peru, I thought the last chance of seeing you married had gone.'

'Gareth?' a familiar voice questioned from the doorway. 'Have you been holding out on me, sweetheart?'

'Not at all.' She cast Cal a glance of welcome over her shoulder. 'It's a tale which has grown in the telling. Gareth left England to study; it had nothing to do with me.'

'Hmm.' Her father's blue eyes twinkled. 'I'm afraid Sara has a bit of a blind spot with regard to her charms.'

Cal leaned back against the wall near the door, an eyebrow lifting in amused enquiry. He wore a pale grey double-breasted suit, his hands in his trouser pockets, his virile health contrasting with the antiseptic white and lemon of the hospital room. 'Were you seeing him?'

That Sara didn't like the question wasn't masked very well. What an infernal cheek, having this sort of discussion in front of her father!

'I doubt if it comes into the category of what *you* would consider a relationship.' She kept the mockery light but didn't like the way he was looking at her. If he'd been a cat, she would be one agitated mouse. Fortunately, she masked her feelings rather better this time.

'Good.' His voice was a soft purr and then he smiled in a relaxed fashion at George St Clair, who had watched the interchange with interest. 'I think you'll find that Sara's in little doubt about the way she affects me.' Pushing himself away from the wall, he came closer to the woman. 'Gareth,' he growled into her ear, 'had better stay where he is. I don't think we'd get along.'

Turning her face slightly, Sara deposited a conciliatory peck on his cheek for her father's benefit. 'There's no competition,' she cooed, hating the way the scent of his skin and the cool graze of his jaw gave her pleasure.

George St Clair literally beamed. He congratulated Cal and they stayed and chatted about plans for the wedding.

'Was he convinced?' The question caused Sara to moodily return his gaze as they walked to his car.

'Yes, I think so.' She was tired, the pretence taking a lot out of her. 'I don't like lying to him.'

'Do you think he'd prefer the truth?'

'No!' she snapped, blue eyes glittering with ice in their depths. 'One thing I know, he'd rather die than let me go through with this.'

Callum Grant must be good at playing poker; his face revealed little of his thoughts. Opening the door for her, he waited until she was seated before he walked around the car and joined her. Settling into the driver's seat, he took a box out of his pocket and with slow deliberation took out a ring.

'I didn't think I'd put you through the effort of choosing it.' He let the light wink on the diamond. 'Give me your hand.'

She held out her hand in a totally uninterested fashion, swallowing as the cold weight rested on her finger. Cal bent his head and kissed the ring, turning her palm upwards and pressing his lips against it.

'At least I'm making it legal,' he pointed out conversationally. He smiled as she closed her eyes to block him out, his fingers stroking through her hair. 'Once you can control this, Sara, you're going to be one lethal lady.' His lips brushed her temple. 'You need a mate, not some high priest at your altar.'

'I'm not like that!' Her eyes snapped open, their guileless depths absorbing the sight of the dark American.

'How would you know?' He barely kissed her before pulling away. He turned the key in the ignition. 'With you, the whole thing is subliminal. Cheer up, things aren't so bad. At least you find me attractive.'

She turned away, her cheeks flaming. 'I wouldn't breathe the same air if I had any choice in the matter.' Her defiance sounded brittle.

'No, darling,' Callum agreed, a smile curving his mouth at the malevolent glare she sent him.

June Douglas, Beatrice Pagett and Angela Carter waited impatiently as the designer finished making the final adjustments to the bridal gown. Teresa Cortez had insisted on going with Cal to have his suit fitted, much to his irritation. She considered it unlucky for the groom's family to see the dress before the wedding and had deliberately absented herself from the house so she wouldn't be tempted. Sara finally came out of the dressing-room to see Angela's wicked smile and Mrs Pagett definitely dewy-eyed.

June Douglas nodded. 'Perfect. It makes you look a little fey.' She viewed the ivory silk taffeta gown.

'Very virginal,' Angela teased her friend. 'He'll break his neck getting down the aisle.'

'It's beautiful,' Mrs Pagett rounded off the chorus of approval. 'I've never seen such a lovely dress.'

Sara thanked them. Her misgivings about the dress were legion. Wearing it made her nervous. It was like the ring on her finger, another link in the chain binding her to Cal.

'Where's Michelle?' Angela queried. Michelle Barron had designed the dress. She was a friend and had made a name for herself in fashion design. 'She's not still terrorising the bridesmaids, is she?'

'No, my pageboy.' Sara grinned. Little Martin Pearson was refusing to try on his outfit. Her bridesmaids came from various families working for St Clair's. One little girl had begged to be a bridesmaid and before she knew it Sara had recruited six. They were all between the ages of five and nine and couldn't wait to get into the lacy, frilly concoctions, sprinkled with rosebuds. Even Angela thought they looked sweet when they made their appearance a little while later. Martin had been cajoled into his suit and joined the girls, inching over to Sara and getting a cuddle for being good.

'I think you look very handsome,' she whispered in his ear, and he giggled.

Angela stayed for lunch and Sara poured her a glass of wine and made a sweeping gesture with her hand. The restaurant was full but they had a table discreetly positioned and couldn't be overheard. 'You have the floor.'

'Sorry?' Angela looked puzzled.

'I have the feeling you want to say something.' She glanced at her watch. 'You're usually at the gallery by now. I don't think it's the wedding paraphernalia that's keeping you from your work.'

Her friend gave her a reluctant nod, acknowledging her perception. 'Well——' she drew out the word '——I—it's just that, well, when you stayed last week, you remember you went to bed before Daniel and me? Your car was parked outside, and who should stop by but——'

'Stephen Appleton.'

'Are you reading my mind?' the dark girl demanded, her exasperation evident.

Sara smiled, appreciating her friend's concern. 'No,

I saw him too. Cal had some papers he wanted my father to sign. Naturally, he wanted to discuss them with me first. He asked Stephen to find me. I didn't tell Mrs Pagett where I was going so when he saw the car on his way home he stopped and checked that it was mine. He thought Cal might want to get in touch with me early the next morning.'

Angela Carter nodded. 'I see.' She didn't look totally convinced. 'It's rather unusual for you not to tell Mrs Pagett where you're going. You're usually very conscientious.'

'Yes, I should have been more considerate,' Sara agreed, closing the subject. Cal, she recalled, had been dismissive about Stephen Appleton's intrusion upon her privacy.

'If you spend a night away from home, I want to know where you are.' He had made his position clear. 'That car should be in the scrapyard; I don't like you driving it.'

Sara had been distracted into a defence of her car and the issue had been lost.

The first day of June greeted the dawn with powder-blue skies and a primrose-coloured sun that strengthened to molten gold as the day grew older.

Sara viewed the rolling lawns and neat flower-beds with a deep-rooted sense of familiarity and love. The window-seat in her bedroom overlooked the rear of St Clair's, the white wood and glass of the conservatory catching the sun, the window-panes dazzling the eye. Below, the house was a hive of activity. One of the glossy house magazines was covering the wedding and everyone was putting in a magnificent effort to show St Clair's at its best.

A quiet knock at the door heralded Mrs Pagett. 'The prisoner's last breakfast,' Sara mused darkly. She smiled and thanked the woman, knowing that the wedding was more of an event for Mrs Pagett than it was for herself.

'Try and eat something,' Beatrice Pagett urged, her voice holding a quiet hush of approval at wedding nerves. Sara had lost weight over the last month and her beauty had an added fragility that June Douglas had labelled 'fey'. The cream silk pyjamas she wore were sleeveless and enhanced the slender line of her arm from shoulder to wrist. The older woman wondered if she wasn't just a little too thin, but then she supposed it was the fashion.

Taking her orange juice from the tray, Sara returned her gaze to the garden when Mrs Pagett left. For the next two days she was surplus to requirements as far as St Clair's was concerned. The time yawned ahead, filled with dreaded obstacles, none of which she anticipated with enthusiasm.

Glancing at her watch, she saw that it was barely nine. She would leave it another hour before she called her father. George St Clair had been transferred from hospital to a private nursing home for convalesence. He was to spend a few hours at St Clair's and insisted on giving Sara away. She thought she might be spared that mockery but no, for Callum Grant the sun shone, her father would risk his health and she would say the expected words as if she meant them.

'Damn you!' The words came from between clenched teeth. She wanted to run. Her sapphire-blue eyes were hectic with half-formed plans. All were to no avail. Tradition, duty, daughterly love, all conspired to dictate her fate. Privileges of birth brought responsibilities too.

Getting up, she went into the bathroom, shedding the silk pyjamas as she went. Her skin felt hot and she lowered the temperature of the shower, letting the cool spray play on her face. That night, Cal would free her from the persistent nag of desire. It ached in her, wrecking her sleep, making his hated presence necessary. She retreated from every encounter with diminished self-esteem, but the addiction grew and left her increasingly vulnerable to his manipulation.

The day dragged on towards twelve o'clock, the appointed hour. George St Clair was fine. A nurse was to accompany him to make sure he didn't over-exert himself.

Outside, in the grounds, a large marquee was erected. The guest list was huge and many people had been invited to attend the reception, if not the ceremony. Cal lacked close relatives; his father was dead and not much was revealed about his mother, but his friends and business acquaintances made up for it.

Sara was hardly aware of the words she spoke. She felt the swing of the diamond drop earrings and the gold chain of the necklace, that had been her mother's, trickle over her skin from her nape to the exposed cleavage of the off-the-shoulder dress.

Cal's voice made her turn her head. He wore a morning suit, his thick black hair perfectly groomed, his gaze upon her face, taking in every detail. She had expected Stephen Appleton to act as best man but instead Zac MacKenzie, the archaeologist he had chased Spanish gold with, performed the honours.

The wedding-ring joined the diamond and she felt Cal's lips touch hers in the expected salute. Then everything was a madness of confetti. They signed the register and were engulfed by people hugging and kissing them.

'You look lovely, darling.' Her father kissed her cheek. 'I wish your mother could have been here.' They shared a tearful smile before the demands of the day separated them again.

Back at St Clair's, long tables, resplendent with silver and sparkling glass, seated over four hundred people. The children were outside, being catered for with barbecued burgers and sausages. The toasts were made and speeches delivered, Zac MacKenzie hinting that all the anecdotes he knew about Cal weren't quite the sort of thing you mentioned at wedding celebrations.

I'll bet, Sara thought, meeting Cal's eyes. He smiled, reading her thoughts, and brushed some confetti from her hair.

'One thing I can say, with perfect sincerity——' the older man touched Cal's shoulder and reclaimed his attention '—is that I couldn't ask for a better friend. Ladies and gentlemen, the bride and groom.'

Sara was surprised to see that Cal looked rather uncomfortable. Zac MacKenzie had meant what he had said, his voice had revealed that, deepening as if he wasn't used to expressing his feelings in such a way. She reflected with cold humour that it must be a novelty for Cal to hear himself praised after the barrage of insults she had poured on his head.

Her father made a short and gentle speech before Cal took his turn, performing with ease. He avoided any expression of sentiment that would demand a response from Sara, for which she was grateful. The formalities over, the tension eased marginally. Everyone else seemed to be enjoying themselves, she observed.

'You're quiet,' Cal commented as they circled the floor in the customary waltz, before others joined the area demarcated for dancing.

'Does that surprise you?' Her eyes were dark pools of pain as they lifted to his, her skin almost as pale as the ivory silk of her dress.

His mouth firmed with anger but his gaze held an element of concern. When the dance finished, he took her back to her seat and asked one of the catering staff for a cup of tea. Champagne on an empty stomach was not to be recommended. Tea, the panacea for all ills, restored a little colour to her cheeks and somehow she managed to get through the rest of the day.

Cal listened to the sounds of singing and revelry drifting up from the grounds. Many of the guests had travelled from London and were staying overnight at the house or at March Haverling. Breathing in the warm summer air, he thought about St Clair's, the wedding, the tradition and formality of it all. An image of sun and dangerous seas, modern-day pirates circling like sharks, came to him. How Zac had acted as decoy, while he swam until his lungs felt like bursting. A flash of white teeth showed in a triumphant smile. He liked a challenge. And he'd certainly got one, he realised when Sara returned from the shower firmly wrapped in nightdress and gown.

'Pity you vetoed the honeymoon. I get the impression you would have liked to get away from this place.'

'Not the place,' she corrected coldly, 'you.' Sara joined him, feeling that that was better than climbing self-consciously into bed. Cal, she observed, was perfectly relaxed.

'You wore less at the wedding.' He regarded her critically.

The nightdress and gown, in matching pale pink, provided a flattering contrast for the silver-blonde hair that fell to her shoulders, but had been bought with St Clair's in mind. The gown, when belted, revealed no more than a triangle of Sara's upper chest. Cal had removed his morning coat and waistcoat. The cravat had remained in remarkably good condition considering what usually happened to his ties. He tugged it free, watching her as he did so. The disdainful sweep of her gaze was outright provocation and he kept his temper with a visible effort.

'They're not going to charge up the stairs at midnight, are they? Tradition's all right in its place, but——'

'Very amusing.' The air was as heady as wine. It cooled her face and toyed with her hair, making the silk of her gown ripple with its soft breath. She did regret staying at St Clair's. It was as if everyone had bought tickets to see Sara St Clair brought like a lamb to the slaughter. Shivering, she tensed as he closed the windows leading out on to the balcony.

'The champagne's chilled. Do you want some? It might help you to relax.'

'No, thank you.' She tossed her hair back defiantly. 'I don't care to be seduced. Just get on with it. It's been a long day and I'm tired.'

Putting a warning finger against her lips, he shook his head. 'I think it's about time I sweetened that tongue of yours before it gets you into trouble. You want this.' His voice was low, the dark hunger in his eyes drawing her in. 'It's been eating you up for days.' He undid the belt of her robe, his hands sliding over her silk-covered waist, drawing her against the solid wall of his body. His arms closed around her, his lips tracing the curve of her cheek. 'I'm doing you a favour. Someone had to kiss you, Sleeping Beauty, or you might have slept forever.'

'If you're expecting gratitude, hell will freeze over first.' Her voice was husky with feeling. Turning her face away from him, her ear rested against his chest, picking up the strong but rapid beat of his heart.

'We'll see.' He hooked his finger under one of the bootlace straps of her nightdress. 'Is this the first time, Sara?' He drew the thin thread of material down over the curve of her shoulder, the warm stroke of his hand appreciating the perfection of her skin.

'It's what you paid for, isn't it?' She tried to fight the attraction but her shoulder lifted in unconscious pleasure, the heat of his palm sensitising her flesh.

'Not exactly.' He was losing interest in the conversation and so was she. His lips moved over the silvery sheen of her hair. She felt the back of his fingers brush her breast as he began to unbutton his shirt.

'When I first saw you,' his voice was low and

intimate, 'I wanted you. It was as if the whole room emptied. The only colours I saw were the blue of your eyes and the moon-silver of your hair.' Breathing in the scent from her hair, he groaned and pushed it back from her face, his eyes almost black with passion as they took in the apprehension in hers. Distracted, his lashes lowered to the invitation of her naked shoulder and the swift rise and fall of her breasts.

'It shouldn't be like this,' she protested, as he brushed her mouth with his, his hands dispossessing her of her dressing-gown.

'Like what?' He kissed and nuzzled the delicate line of her jaw. 'It feels great to me.'

Sara felt a stab of resentment at the amusement that laced the otherwise husky admission. 'It should mean more than this.' Her voice faltered. Cal didn't seem chastised by her description. His handsome face stilled as he let his fingers trail over her shoulders and down her arms, taking the nightdress with them in one slow movement. The silk rustled to a pool at her feet.

Naked, Sara endured the burn of his eyes over her body. Drawing her close, he captured her reluctant mouth, the heat of his flesh against her breasts flooding her with sensation. Acutely embarrassed and confused by the sensual delight she was experiencing, her response was half a retreat. Cal followed every turn of her head, his hand cupping her jaw, then touching her face, pushing into her hair and gripping a handful, finally stilling her and taking full advantage. Her head fell back and he released his grip and supported her neck with his arm, his kisses gentling, inviting her to return the pressure, biting playfully at her lower lip, parting her mouth with his. Letting his tongue trace the soft inner flesh, he coaxed her into returning his kiss fully, the groan deep in his throat appreciative when she rebuffed and teased the intruder in turn, the fragile barriers of her defence melting away.

Sara's moan of anguished despair was muffled by his lips. For the first time a man had free access to her body. Moreover, it was the man she detested more than any other. Shame at her inability to resist scourged her and deepened as he no longer had to control her. His hands swept down her back and cupped the smooth curves of her buttocks, bringing her into the hard, thrusting power of his hips.

Lifting his head, Cal put his hand at the side of her face, viewing the hot, passionate need mingled with shame and reproach. Sara's lips were pink and swollen from his kisses, her eyes soulful and sexy at the same time. Women of his acquaintance didn't usually possess both qualities. His free hand circled her throat, feeling the pulse there before making the slow journey to her breast. Sara's body jerked at the possessive tightening of his fingers. His grip relaxed and became teasing, his finger and thumb closing over the soft bud of her nipple. She turned her face into his throat with a soft sob.

'Just drown.' He kissed her eyebrow, nuzzling at her ear, his hand taking the weight of her breast, caressing her, enjoying what had previously been only a fleeting intimacy.

Sara was drowning. The tantalising stroke of his fingers made her want more and she was impatient. When his hand swept down to the taut plane of her stomach, Sara caught her breath, her arms winding around his neck, her mouth searching for his. Wildfire ran through her blood. Her fingers buried themselves in his hair and then, gripping his shoulders, she almost howled with frustration as he explored the curve of her hips and the tight line of her waist.

'Oh, please, Cal, it's driving me crazy.' She couldn't help the words tumbling from her lips.

He met the uplift of her face, his kiss accepting her whispered desire, his caresses becoming increasingly intimate until her fervency made him pick her up and place her on the bed.

Later, the rustle of sheets witnessed the heated melding of their bodies as they drove for release. Cal's mouth fastened on the darkened crest of her breast, his urgent, hungry movements making her hips writhe restlessly. Sara opened her mouth against the dark silk of his hair, breathing, tasting him, her lips eager as he raised his head, his arms straining as they took his weight. The lean hunger of his body arched over hers. She was surrounded by him, her head nestling between his arms, his mouth on hers, his hips pinning her to the bed. Yet her desire for escape was gone. She had escaped to a dark, hot jungle where the rhythm of life was supreme. Deeper and deeper, she plunged into the heart of primeval heat, and then it hit her. The coil of tension tightened unbearably until she cried out with the joyous agony of it. Her eyes widened in wonder, her head twisted to find some coolness that would ease the sparks that showered over her.

Cal's head bent, his shoulders gleaming with sweat. A sweet gladness ran through him as he felt the innocent eagerness of her body wrap itself around him. Knowing that he could no longer hurt her, he gave rein to the intensely passionate nature he possessed.

'Sara.' Cal eased away from her some time later, a smile touching his mouth at the totally abandoned picture she made. Not wanting to disturb the blissful dream she was in, he pulled her gently against his chest. Refusing to speak, she sought the harbour of his arms, feeling as if she wanted to stay there forever.

CHAPTER SIX

BACK in her workshop the next morning, Sara put a new batch of St Clair's replicas on the bench in front of her and began to paint furiously. It was Sunday. The house was in the hands of June Douglas. The weekends were always the peak time for tourists and it was business as usual. As if on cue, June knocked briefly and entered, a questioning look on her face.

'Mrs Pagett said I'd find you in here. Don't you ever stop work?'

'Habit,' she muttered. 'It's my way of relaxing.' Sara didn't feel very talkative. 'What can I do for you?' Her attention was given for a moment before she took up her paintbrush.

'Mr Grant's car is parked in one of the spaces usually left for coaches. It's Ashton's, and they're very good business. Normally, I wouldn't bother you but——'

'Why don't you ask him to move it?' She concentrated hard as she painted the windows.

'Well—Mrs Pagett seems to think he's still in bed.' June looked amused as Sara's head shot up.

'Oh.' Putting the latest miniature down carefully, she wiped her hands on her dungarees. It was nearly eleven. What was he doing still in bed? He might as well advertise the fact——Embarrassment tortured her. Unlike him, she had been unable to sleep, finally achieving freedom around dawn when Cal had been too tired to use his own particular form of restraint.

89

Being asked to get his car keys was akin to an escaped Christian's being asked to re-enter the lion's den.

Hands in pockets, she left the workshop, promising to move the car herself. Using the old servants' stairs, she avoided the people touring the house and entered the private quarters.

Approaching the bedroom, she took a deep breath and entered, relieved to find the bed empty. The sound of the shower in the adjoining room revealed his presence. Sara's eyes skidded around the room, avoiding the rumpled sheets. She saw his car keys on the bedside cabinet and quickly crossed the room. Sweeping them up, she hastily made for the door.

'Morning, Sara.' His voice stopped her in her tracks.

'Oh—er—hello.' She felt totally inadequate to the situation, thinking hello sounded ridiculously formal, but her mind had blanked out and she fought against babbling something equally banal about the weather.

Cal took in her discomposure with a knowledgeable glint in his eyes. The dungarees were noted, as was her inability to meet his gaze. Then, as if to confound him, her chin lifted and the pride he had thought vanquished re-established itself. Perhaps pride was the wrong word for it, he mused; she had a dignity about her that made him feel a kingsize rat. Callum Grant had his own code of ethics which he did not break; Sara was one of the few people who could make him feel uncomfortable about himself. He didn't like the feeling, and attack was the best form of defence.

'When did you get up?' Cal subjected her to a rather unnerving appraisal. 'I missed you.'

'I—er—I'd better go.' She had rediscovered blushing since his abrupt intrusion into her life and was developing it into an art form.

'Coming back?' The question was designed to provoke her, and succeeded.

'No, I'm not.' She was unwillingly aware of the lean strength of his body. The black hair on his chest was wet from the shower and flattened back against his tanned skin, feathering out from a dark line starting at his breastbone and disappearing beneath the skimpy towel, low on his hips. 'Did you have to sleep so late? Everyone will think——'

'We're on our honeymoon,' he supplied easily.

Hot-eyed, she swallowed drily as he approached. 'There's a coach full of people——'

'There must be other places to visit.' He was teasing her, but the deliberate placing of his hands against the door, trapping her with his arms, brought back memories of the night before.

'I thought you were trying to get this place into the black.' He was too close, the power of his personality beating down the barriers she had hastily tried to erect. Cal watched her intently and she drew on unknown reserves of determination to fight the panic flooding through her.

'You're right,' he agreed, openly mocking her. 'Business comes first.' He nodded with approval, moving back. 'You'll make a good wife.'

'I absolutely loathe you,' she muttered, turning quickly and leaving the room.

Loathing was only one of her emotional reactions towards Callum Grant. She felt extremely vulnerable after their night together. It was dreadful to feel so utterly out of her depth.

Sara's blue eyes glowed with an inner heat. Even now, when she was tired and angry, the sight of him

half naked made her senses prickle uncomfortably. Cal
had made her body his ally.

Her love for her father had put her into Cal's power
and she had despised him for the emotional blackmail
he had used to make her agree to the marriage. Cal,
she realised, had been biding his time. The mocking
amusement that witnessed her tantrums was fuelled by
the foreknowledge of what was to come. Sara had
thought herself her own woman, independent of men;
Cal had seen passionate need unfulfilled.

Sara made her way back down the servants' stairs,
her brain working frantically. She almost wished she
had hated every minute in his arms. Almost, but not
quite. She trembled as she recalled the stroke of his
strong brown fingers, moving at will over the fairness
of her skin. She had been held in a spell of silence
where touch was the only language. The hunger raging
in him had the fierce blaze of a white-hot flame.
Uncontrolled, he could have hurt her, she knew that.
Was that why she had allowed him to tease her senses
into an answering flame? Scrupulously honest, Sara
denied herself that refuge. Haunting, almost subliminal
memories of her fingers clawing the sheet as he found
the sensitive core of her womanhood decried such
flimsy excuses. Brought down to the basics, she was in
need of a mate and had the misfortune to find Callum
Grant powerfully attractive.

Cal, she sensed, had deliberately set out to teach her
a lesson. Her eagerness to learn had surprised them
both. Vague memories of Cal's huskily spoken desires
and groans of pleasure as she complied hinted at a
power within her grasp she had yet to fully understand.
In time, she comforted herself, she would gain some

control over the way she felt, Cal had said so himself. That did nothing to reassure her. To be able to deal with her husband on equal terms, she wouldn't recognise herself.

The tourists in their coach were intrigued and forgot their fifteen-minute wait to park. They had been told about the wedding as part of the tourist package, and the sight of the bride of one day removing her husband's car from the car park captivated them enough to set cameras clicking. It only increased Sara's sense of paranoia. Remaining the same shade of scarlet, she parked the car around the back of St Clair's and wondered what to do next. She thirsted for normality, when all around her were determined that she should have the day free.

Stephen Appleton arrived to give Callum Grant an update on his business affairs and found himself following Cal around the house, apparently speaking to deaf ears.

'And I decided to put down a fifty-million deposit on Mars as a future investment,' he tested the water, sure his employer was in another realm. Cal merely smiled and continued to stalk his prey.

'Are you listening to a word I say—sir? You seem rather distracted.'

'You can say that again,' the American murmured but didn't seem too bothered about it.

'Sara's certainly——' The words were swallowed at Callum Grant's sudden sharpening of attention. 'Very beautiful,' he ameliorated. He was reprieved by the woman in question almost bumping into them in the main hall, and watched the two protagonists with interest.

Sara was extremely flustered as the coach party she had made way for crossed her path like a waddle of remote-control ducklings. She smiled vaguely at them and wished the ground would open up and swallow her.

'Have you had your breakfast, Sara?' In truth, she hadn't been able to eat a thing, but it was nearly lunchtime! 'You look pale, honey.' He seemed to be enjoying himself. How he could say she looked pale when her face was a permanant beacon was beyond her. What she did know was that the main hall was far from private.

'I'll tell you what, we'll call it lunch and I'll take you out. You could do with a break from this place.' Assuming her agreement, he turned to Appleton. 'Steve, don't page me unless it's something to do with Sara's father,' he said, and thus removed the obstacle she was about to fling in his path. Sara stood beside him, feeling his arm go around her waist.

'I think these things——' he flicked a careless hand at her dungarees '—should go out with the garbage.'

'I'll change,' she volunteered, hot-footing it to the bedroom before he had the chance to follow her, quickly choosing a cool summer dress to match the casual beige shirt and cream trousers Cal had opted for.

Despite her antipathy towards her husband, she was glad, for once, to be leaving the environs of St Clair's. Opening the car door for her, Cal saw her seated and then joined her, his thigh brushing hers as he fastened his safety-belt and cast a glance at Sara's. She glared at him.

'I am capable of fastening my own seatbelt,' she snapped.

'The last person to use that harness was Zac; you're not exactly the same size.'

It was slack. With difficulty, she adjusted it and he started up the car without another word on the subject.

'Tired?' His deep voice had an intimate note to it. 'You can't have slept much.'

'I didn't sleep at all.' She wanted to sound dismissive but instead her voice had a childish, resentful sound to it.

A slow smile greeted her discomfort. 'I don't know how you kept awake——'

'I don't want to talk about it!' She was suddenly furious. 'I know it gives you a great deal of pleasure to make fun out of me.' His widening grin didn't cool her mood. 'I suppose it's too much to ask, to expect any sensitivity from you!'

'Sara,' he drawled. 'After all we shared——All right,' he acknowledged the impotent sound of frustration she made. 'You don't want to talk. Sit back. Relax. I'll drive for a while.'

Searching his profile for ulterior motives, she gradually calmed as he showed signs of being true to his word, putting on a cassette of contemporary jazz, and concentrating on his driving.

Heavy-eyed, she gazed out over the familiar fields. Hampshire was one of the 'garden counties' serving London. In the old days, it would have fed the busy throng of the metropolis—still did to a degree, but its ever-growing export was commuters. Commuters and computers; her thoughts came back to Callum Grant. She supposed that if he hadn't been a foreigner, he would epitomise the modern trend. Eventually, her eyelids drooped and Sara's head found Cal's shoulder as sleep claimed her.

Sara awoke to find herself on a car rug in a quiet countryside meadow. Puzzled, she sat up, her features sleep-flushed, her eyes widening as she recognised Cal. He appeared to be fishing. What he was actually doing was retrieving a bottle of wine from the chill depths of a stream.

'Sleeping Beauty awakes,' he said as he turned. 'It's a little late for lunch, so I decided on a picnic.' Removing the foil from the bottle, he glanced at her. 'You look better, anyway. Not quite so uptight. Strange.' His voice was reflective. 'I thought I'd got rid of the tension last night. I guess you feel guilty about the way I make you feel. I don't know why, it's a good feeling.'

She joined him by the edge of the stream, scooping up some water and cooling her face with it. It occurred to her that Cal preferred a combative relationship to a more placid one. Ever eager to please, she obliged him.

'You're not my idea of a husband.' She accepted his handkerchief and dried her face.

'No?' He stroked a finger over her shoulder. 'Who is? Some Hooray Henry with a landed estate.'

She met his gaze, equal to the challenge there. 'You think I'm a snob?' she confronted him. 'Out to redress the family fortunes? I'm afraid you're quite wrong. I wouldn't have wanted your money or anyone else's. I'm confident I could manage on my own.'

'Maybe.' He uncorked the bottle with easy strength.

'What about Gareth Haldane? Wasn't he the right type?'

She got up, avoiding the question. Let him think what he liked. If she explained that no man had ever set her heart racing, he could only be flattered into thinking he did. It was anger, irritation, sexual inexperience that made her react so strongly to him.

Walking back to the rug, she was aware of his quiet tread behind her. She was unusually attuned to him. His presence seemed to alert every nerve in her body, making her skin prickle uncomfortably.

Sara was surprised to find she was hungry and enjoyed the picnic. He had bought several cheeses, a French stick and some olives from a delicatessen. Cal ate without any real interest, his thoughts clearly elsewhere. She was licking a breadcrumb from the side of her mouth when she discovered where. Their eyes collided and suddenly the meadow seemed very quiet and the sun shattered into a million splinters and entered Sara's blood. She felt the weight of his body as a physical thing, when in fact he didn't move but continued to hold her gaze.

'I didn't hurt you, did I, sweetheart?' He touched the side of her face. 'That wasn't why you couldn't sleep?'

'No.' She shook her head, the undiluted concern he showed demanding honesty from her. She was reluctant to discuss such a personal subject with him. Sara considered their physical relationship was a night-time affair and disliked his habit of dragging it out into the daylight.

'So.' He brushed a few remaining specks of bread

away with his thumb. 'You just couldn't bear to sleep with me. Is that it?'

'No, I don't know—I was over-tired, I suppose.' Why she was stumbling for an explanation, she didn't know. 'I'm not used to—being with you.' Her lips got heavier as she made the husky admission and she spoke the end of the sentence against his mouth.

It was a nice kiss, warm and lazy, only a hint of demand in the way he broke from her mouth and then returned as if he had realised how sweet it was and wanted to protract the tender moment.

Public displays were strictly against Sara's code of ethics. A polite peck on the cheek and linked arms was as far as she had previously been prepared to go. This reserve had, no doubt, enhanced her virginal reputation. Her friends who had gone through a similar education had taken delight in rebelling rather spectacularly.

'There's no one around.' Cal guessed the reason for the rigidity of her body. 'When I have time——' he kissed her nose and grinned at her surprised expression '—we'll go somewhere hot. Your father can come with us if necessary.' A wicked gleam in his eyes acknowledged the fact that Sara was inclined to use George St Clair as a cross against his perceived darkness. Picking a daisy, he trailed it along the curve of her cheek, watching its progress and then studying the confused, slightly resentful blue of her eyes. 'You could just enjoy it,' he suggested, mocking her discomfort.

'I'm not the abandoned type.' She watched the humour light his eyes and a vision of her limbs entwined with his, her mouth open against his throat, made her lashes sweep downwards to shut him out.

'I wouldn't say that,' he provoked her, the daisy brushing across the parting of her lips. 'But then your secret's safe with me.'

That anything would be remotely safe with him she very much doubted. She was aware of him moving away from her and her eyes widened as she saw him unbuttoning his shirt. Sara swallowed drily. His physique was impressive, if you liked that sort of thing. His Latin skin-tone, height and long, muscled limbs were a virile combination of Spanish and Celt ancestry. He, she was quite sure, would be perfectly happy turning the green of an English meadow into a kingsize bed.

'I don't know what you're thinking about,' he murmured, without looking at her. 'But your eyes are doing terrible things to my libido.'

'Don't flatter yourself,' she snapped, scrambling to her feet. 'I'm going for a walk.'

Cal watched her go, admiring her slender grace, his mouth tilting into a regretful smile. Yawning, he packed away the remains of the picnic and then stretched out on the rug, his shirt falling back from his ribcage to rest at his sides. Usually it took him a long time to unwind, but Sara's company both stimulated and relaxed him. Memories of the previous evening kept him pleasantly occupied, while Sara tried to find some peace in the very Englishness of her surroundings.

Sara found getting back to the daily grind of St Clair's a mixed blessing. She didn't feel normal. Everything about the house was the same but changed slightly by Cal's presence. The staff now extended their loyalty and respect to him and were relieved that their jobs had been reprieved from the constant threat of the St Clair finances. Repairs that had been put off on numerous occasions had been costed and a succession of workmen were permanently in residence.

'It must be a relief to get the old place smartened up,' June Douglas commented as they tried to keep the tours and restaurant free of dust and left in peace from the sporadic hammering.

'Yes.' Sara smiled briefly, studying their latest plan dealing with the central heating to be put in. 'I think we should think about broadening the menu for the restaurant. If we're increasing our catering, we should think about being a little more adventurous.'

'Mmm, why not?'

'We haven't got an open cheque-book.' She tried to stem the view that Cal's presence should affect their normal economies. 'We'll still have to budget. I'm——' she cleared her throat '—thinking of doing a business course. I shall be in control of St Clair's management when my father returns, and I want to make sure I do things properly.'

She was surprised later to discover that Cal approved of her decision. 'Why not?' he drawled. 'I'll help you with your homework.'

'I have a degree in fine arts and music,' she informed him icily, meaning that she was quite capable of managing without his help.

'That should be useful.' He viewed her through a blue haze from the thin cigar he was smoking, polluting the hitherto untainted air in her private parlour.

It annoyed her the way he made himself comfortable in her sanctuary. Most evenings, when he was free, he would join her there. Lounging on the couch, its fresh, flowery print an incongruous setting for his very male presence, he dominated the room. He wore jeans and a royal blue T-shirt that lovingly moulded the muscles of his chest. His feet were bare, propped negligently on the opposite end of the couch.

'I'm hot,' he complained, pushing his hand under his T-shirt, exposing his stomach to the air, idly fingering his ribcage. To Sara's less liberated mind, he was an appalling exhibitionist, purposely distracting her from working on the new menu.

Putting her pen in her mouth, she tapped her teeth, her expression thoughtful. Copying his indolent way of looking at her, she let her gaze wander over his body. When she reached his face, the invitation to do more than look wasn't subtly expressed. Unable to beat him at that particular game, she asked him something that had been bothering her.

'Why didn't your mother attend the wedding?' She surprised him with the question and his eyes hardened, the shutters coming down.

'I haven't any idea.' He drew on the cigar he was smoking, blowing a stream of smoke up at the ceiling.

Sara was curious. She could ask Teresa, but that would expose how little she knew of his background.

'Is it a sensitive subject?' she asked, despite the 'keep off the grass' signs being posted.

'It could be because,' he said consido^ingly, 'I didn't invite her. She wasn't a very good mother, I gave Teresa the job, and pensioned her off.' A smile curled his mouth but he didn't look amused.

'Oh.' She pretended to be inspired. 'If I'm not a very good wife, will you do the same for me?'

A weighty silence developed between them. 'If

you're not a very good wife, you won't need a pension.'
The threat was meant to be taken seriously. The
brooding quality to his gaze made her shiver.

'Tell me about her,' she invited, sensing that his
mother was central to his attitude to women. Sara
herself had a reason for entering a loveless marriage;
she was intrigued to know his.

'No,' he refused point-blank.

'Why?'

'Because it isn't necessary for you to know.'

'I see.' She was hurt, and annoyed for feeling that
way. Sara was beginning to cope with the demands of
her marriage and her newly found womanhood, but
not the emotional desert that went with them. Their
nights together were dreams of sensual enchantment.
She slept in his arms and felt happy there, but come
the next morning the tenderness disappeared and at
best they co-existed, more usually scoring points off
each other in a manner that gave Sara very little
pleasure when she reflected on it later in the day.

'I'd rather you didn't smoke in here,' she needled
him, needing an outlet for the pain which was surprisingly intense. If he refused to share with her, she had
no intention of putting up with his bad habits. 'This is
my room. There are plenty of others you can pollute.'

Glancing around the cluttered parlour, he stood up.
'Are you getting a grant for this course, honey?'

She had the feeling he already knew the answer to
that one. 'I thought you could write it off against tax,'
she suggested brightly.

'I suppose you could.' He went to the door. 'If this
place made a profit. If you remember, Sara, St Clair's
doesn't belong to me; all I can write off are the business

expenses in line with our agreement. You can have your room back.' He made a sweeping gesture. 'I won't come in unless you ask. Oh——' He touched his forehead in a rather staged act of forgetfulness. 'I guess it'll be OK for the workmen to fix the chimney and repair the brickwork under the window?'

'Quite all right.' Blue eyes met his dark gaze, recognising the anger there but not able to back down. 'If you want an inventory of what you've bought, Cal, it comes down to a hostess for your guests and my sleeping with you—at night,' she added hastily, not liking the hard glitter in his eyes.

'And for these considerations on your part——' he came back into the room '—I supply the money to keep this place going.'

'A loan,' she specified, her chin tilting proudly. 'I intend to pay you back.'

'That isn't necessary.'

'I think it is.' She remained stubborn.

His jaw squared ominously. 'I'll tell David to keep the receipts.'

Sara watched him go and wondered why victory should make her feel so hollow.

The endless round of dinner parties, with the recruitment of two new members of staff, became an extension of the restaurant catering. The only extra demand was on Sara, who had to exercise her skills as a conversationalist—and with some of Cal's business acquaintances skill was certainly required.

That night, the table in the long dining-room looked suitably impressive. Several large Gothic candelabra took pride of place. Slim white candles provided a host of small flames, charmingly reflected upon crystal and silver. The Coalport dinner service evinced a discreet and decorative twentieth-century influence. The first course was a choice between *beignets de Camembert* with a selection of puréed fruits or spiced watercress soup.

Sara was unaware of the stunning contrast made by her silver-blonde hair and the midnight-blue evening dress, encrusted with minute beads. It was felt by more than one person there that she deserved better than the conversation with her partner, enlisting her opinions on what he should buy his wife for her birthday and what was involved in joining the local hunt.

Sara's eyes met Cal's but there was no camaraderie or sympathy there. It was what she was being paid for; he expected efficiency from his staff. Cal was certainly keeping his own high standards, she reflected sourly, watching him charm an attractive brunette in a flame-red dress. She wondered if he would appreciate it if she showed the same enthusiasm for her work.

Later that evening, when Cal deigned to dance with her, she noticed that the brunette in the red dress was watching them with evident interest.

'Who is she?' Sara asked bluntly. 'She can't take her eyes off you.'

'Bianca Shannon.' He had his back to his admirer but had no difficulty in identifying whom she meant.

'An old friend?' She raised an eyebrow, but found herself not wanting to hear the answer.

'Her husband does a lot of business with one of my companies. He was suffering from jet lag, and Bianca advised him to rest.'

'He's older, no doubt,' she drew her own conclusions.

Cal gave her a dry look. 'You're not suggesting she married him for his money, are you? That *would* be unusual.'

'I didn't marry you for your money.' Sara's voice was low and hurt. 'I married you because that was the only way I could ensure my father's peace of mind.'

'Yes, I know.' He went quiet and they danced silently to the slow, melancholic music being played. When the last strains of the melody died, Cal thanked her, his eyes moving past her in search of someone. 'I'll be late tonight.' The ironic, 'Don't wait up,' stung.

Sara watched him join a circle of his business associates, smiling briefly as another grey-haired executive distracted her with the request for the next waltz. Her feet mechanically went through the movements but inside she felt sick and miserable. All sorts of wild schemes were concocted in her mind, all having the same result, making her husband feel as unhappy as she did. It struck her like a thunderbolt. She was jealous! The revelation made her go cold all over. It had to be faced, she didn't want him touching anyone else. She couldn't sleep under the same roof, knowing he was with another woman.

It was something of an anticlimax to discover that Cal was taking a mixed party to the casino. Bianca Shannon had reluctantly returned to her husband and was not among their number.

Cal noticed the paleness of her face and came to her side, excusing himself from the throng at the door. 'Are you all right?' His hand briefly tested her forehead. 'You look as if——' He was right. Making a muffled apology, she raced for the nearest bathroom. Cal apologised to his guests and handed them over to Stephen Appleton.

'Make sure they get everything they want,' he instructed, his eyes flicking to the corridor Sara had disappeared down.

'Cal, Walter Durkin——'

'I'll see him tomorrow.'

The young Englishman shook his head, a reluctant smile breaking out on his features.

'Where the hell did you get to?' Cal demanded as she returned to their bedroom. 'This house is crazy; I was sure you'd gone down to the west wing.'

'I used the servants' stairs.' She sat down on the bed and he came round to her, going down on one knee and looking up into her face.

'Do you want me to call a doctor? You still look pale.'

'No.' She shook her head tiredly. 'I'm all right. I thought you were going to the casino.'

'Forget that.' He took hold of her chin. 'You've been acting strangely all evening. What's the matter?' Dark eyes searched her face. 'I don't think you eat enough— and maybe you don't get enough sleep, huh?' His smile was nice.

'I feel better.' She was warmed by his concern.

He didn't look convinced. 'I'll put you to bed. Where's your nightdress?'

'You told me not to buy one,' she reminded him, her lips tilting as he fought to keep his features immobile.

'You should always have a nightdress for emergencies,' he informed her gravely. 'And I'm sure a nice girl like you has one just to impress the domestic staff.'

She laughed and directed him towards the correct drawer. Perfectly capable of undressing herself, she let him do it, rather enjoying the novelty of Cal in a caring mood. She had already washed her face and cleaned her teeth to make herself feel better, and slipped between the sheets when he pulled the covers back for her. Looking unusually indecisive, he pushed his hand through his hair.

'Maybe it would be better if you slept alone. If you draw me a map, I'll find a spare room——'

'No,' she forestalled him. 'I mean—there aren't any, not ready, anyway.'

Giving her a long look, he nodded. Disappearing into the bathroom, he came back naked and pulled on a pair of black briefs.

'You're looking better,' he commented on the tinge of colour in her cheeks. Getting in beside her, he settled his long limbs against hers. Sara turned into him wordlessly, her face against his chest, breathing in his clean scent.

'Is something bothering you?' he asked again, stroking her hair.

Sara felt she wouldn't know where to start. To suffer the pain of jealousy over a man whom, a month before, she could have wished off the face of the earth, was devastating enough. Discovering that passionate attachment involved such a gamut of emotions was a total revelation. Love, she expected, had such torments but to feel so mixed up when all she and Cal had in common was mutual sexual gratification struck fear into her heart. There was nothing she could do to protect herself against such pain. Cal had no reason to remain faithful to her. Part of the convenience of their marriage, for him, was that it left him free to do what he liked.

'Sara?' he questioned her silence, smoothing her hair away from her face.

She pretended to be asleep and felt his breath on her cheek before he kissed her softly. Sara despised herself for the happiness the caress brought. It would burn itself out, she comforted herself. . .one day.

CHAPTER SEVEN

'GARETH!' Stephen Appleton greeted his old friend warmly, a slight shadow crossing his face when he remembered Haldane's interest in Sara Grant, née St Clair. Gareth had been in Peru for six months. In terms of his own love life that seemed a lifetime, and he hoped the grand passion had subsided.

'Hello, Stephen. What do you think of the tan?'

'Very impressive.' He smiled at the red-headed six-footer. 'I'm not sure it's a tan, though. I think your freckles have joined up.' Stephen Appleton glanced at the dinner suit. Gareth had never been over-keen to 'dress up', and casinos weren't one of his usual haunts either.

'Developed a taste for gambling?'

'Hardly. I heard the St Clairs spend a lot of time up here these days, and I wanted to see Sara.'

'Er—Sara—you haven't been home yet, then? Heard the news?'

'No.' Gareth looked cheerful and a little bit embarrassed. 'I'm not due back for another week, but once I'd made the decision to come back it seemed pointless to hang on. I know that George has been gambling—he's got himself into a bit of a hole by all accounts, and I intend to help Sara out any way I can. No one was in when I got home, so I came on here.'

'I see.' Stephen ordered two double Scotches. 'You're a bit behind the times. I suppose the post must take quite a while.' He cleared his throat, not relishing his task. 'Come and sit down, Gareth. I think there's something you should know.'

Alarm spread across Gareth Haldane's features. He followed Stephen to a table and recoiled in horror when his friend broke the news.

'Callum Grant!' Gareth could hardly believe his ears. 'That playboy! How could Sara possibly see anything in him? He's nothing more than a financial streetfighter.'

'He's actually a very astute businessman,' Stephen Appleton mediated. 'Keep your voice down, half the people here are his guests.'

'I don't care.' Gareth was shaking, his skin red under his tan.

'Well, I do—he's my boss. Look, Gareth, we're old friends, I'll give you some good advice. Don't get in Grant's way. Sara can fight her own battles, believe me.'

'Sara, with someone like that! I can't believe it.'

'Oh, I don't know.' Stephen Appleton had his eye on Walter Durkin; he wasn't particularly diplomatic. 'Women find him very attractive. He's also as rich as Croesus. Most of Sara's set are mad with envy.'

Gareth shook his head, swallowing his whisky as if he needed it. 'There's more to it. I know Sara. This is all very sudden; that's not like her.'

Stephen shrugged. Callum Grant had knocked Miss Prim and Proper sideways as far as he could see, and as an interested observer he thought Sara's bout of illness had more to do with jealousy than anything she had eaten that night. He was sensitive enough not to divulge domestic details of the couple to Gareth Haldane. No doubt Gareth would see them together and realise he was on a losing wicket.

'Sorry to give you the bad news. I've got to get back to work. Give me a ring, we'll go out on the town.' Getting up, he went in pursuit of the American businessman Cal would want him to impress. He'd have to tell his employer about Gareth; he just hoped his friend had the sense to give up the chase.

Sunlight warmed Sara's skin, a gentle breeze from the window stirring her hair. She awoke, a faint smile on her face as she felt a warm hand move over her hip. The satin of her apricot lingerie clung to Cal's fingers and she held her breath as the sheets rustled and he moved closer, his body warming her back.

'Sara?' His voice was low, testing her response, his fingers spreading over her stomach. 'It's nine o'clock,' he murmured into her hair. 'I'm supposed to have a breakfast meeting with Steve.'

'You'll be late,' she whispered, her stomach muscles tensing as he drew teasing patterns around her navel.

'I was late an hour ago.'

'Oh, and what happens at nine?' She smiled against the pillowslip as his mouth nuzzled the join of her neck.

'I play golf,' he muttered in a tone of disgust. 'I really can't keep avoiding Walter Durkin, he'll develop a complex.'

Turning into his arms, she kissed him softly. 'You were very kind last night, thank you.'

'Almost like a husband?' His dark eyes were warm as they searched the depths of hers. Reaching up for him, she drew his head down to her. Cal's mouth moved over hers with quickly aroused passion, suggesting his night had not been quite as peaceful as hers.

Sara found it all too easy to respond. Bianca Shannon's advent into her life had brought with it sudden feelings of insecurity and a need for reassurance. If Cal was surprised at the spontaneous response, he didn't show it. He fed the eager uptilt of her mouth, his lips returning again and again, his tongue teasing and then demanding.

'You're beautiful,' he whispered. 'It isn't easy sleeping next to you when you're restless.' His words were muffled against her throat but audible. 'You followed me around the bed all night; it took a lot of will-power not to wake you.'

'Why didn't you?' She was learning to be provocative and Cal raised his head, his eyes narrowing suspiciously as her fingers stroked over his stubbled jaw. Some men looked as if they were ill when unshaven; Cal looked mean and sexy.

'The idea was for you to get some sleep,' he reminded her derisively, his jaw lifting slightly as her index finger traced a line under his chin.

'It sounds as if you didn't get much.' Her teasing made his eyes harden.

The insistent buzz of his paging machine broke into the intimacy between them. Cal disentangled himself and moved to pick up the phone. 'I'll be down in ten minutes,' he growled without waiting for a response.

Sara watched him go into the bathroom with a measure of regret that wasn't entirely physical. Cal had been uneasy the moment she had acknowledged her need for him. It hadn't been the first time, but her whispered confessions during their lovemaking were drawn from her by his undoubted skill as a lover. The warmth she had felt towards him that morning had been a response to his tenderness of the night before, and his sudden detachment showed her exactly what Cal wanted from their relationship. Sara had never envisaged herself as a rich man's plaything and had no intention of becoming one.

Cal came back into the room and dressed, pulling on his golfing clothes. He cast a glance in her direction, his face totally unrevealing.

'Wives usually arrive at the club around one. Take anybody who's interested into the village. They can pay extortionate prices for sheepskins, that should keep them happy.'

He was referring to one of the shops in the village dealing exclusively in leather and suede. The 'wives' sounded like a herd of mindless sheep themselves, she mused, and she the shepherdess.

'I'll try and keep them amused.' She was dry. As she sat up, the neckline of her nightdress revealed a tempting glimpse of her breasts, her fair hair tumbled around her shoulders.

'I'd prefer to do business without all this. It wastes time,' he said, picking up on her criticism. 'But it's the name of the game, babe.' He advanced on her, lifting her out of bed, much to her disgust, and depositing her on her feet. 'Lay on that cool English charm and I'll think about sending you back to school.'

Ruffling her hair, he brought her head forward and kissed the crown. The burning look of resentment she sent him made him touch his heart mockingly and then he was gone, leaving Sara feeling flat and depressed.

March Haverling was an old market town. It attracted many city-wearied business folk who wanted a touch of rural life not too far from the bright lights of London. Consequently it was filled with 'quaint' little shops that were exclusive and extremely expensive. They were in the Shepherd's Nook when Stephen Appleton appeared at her shoulder. Sara glanced pointedly at her watch.

'Not late, surely?' she murmured, sarcasm well muted. 'I thought I'd timed it rather well.'

'Cal's losing to Walter Durkin like a true professional,' he grinned at her, 'making up for his absence at the casino. Feeling all right, Sara?'

'Fine.' She watched Ginger Hailey pick up yet another handbag. Stephen's attitude towards her often verged on the conspiratorial. She suspected he admired her for her supposed skill in bringing Cal to the altar. 'I feel much better today; something must have disagreed with me.'

'Mmm. Bianca Shannon, I'd say.' He laughed at her surprised look. 'Sometimes, Sara, you're rather transparent. But it's healthy for you to feel that way about Cal. Gareth's back and he's got some strange idea in his head that you've fallen into the grips of a womanising monster. I suggest you convince him otherwise. Cal isn't particularly tolerant of competition; he only loses when he means to.'

Sara met his eyes, aware that Stephen was trying to guard his own interests and those of his friend at the same time.

'Have you told Cal about Gareth?'

He couldn't lie to her. There was something about her, a certain integrity, that made him feel cheap.

'Yes.' His face flushed. 'He'd find out quickly enough, it's my job to keep him informed.'

'I see.' She intervened when Ginger took her purchases to the counter, negotiating the usual discount. She knew the wealthy women she escorted wouldn't really notice the difference, but after years of stringent economy at St Clair's she disliked seeing money wasted. The shop's profit margin, she knew, was sizeable.

At half-past twelve Sara gathered her party together and saw them into the two limousines.

'You work too hard, honey,' Ginger confided to her in a quiet aside. 'Keeping a man like Cal happy is a full-time job. There's always somebody waiting in the wings.' She glanced at Bianca Shannon without too much subtlety.

Sara viewed a life of shopping and visiting fashion shows with dread. 'I like keeping busy,' she demurred, aware of Bianca Shannon's interest in their conversation even though the woman had never actually spoken to her in person. Bianca appeared to be sulking. Either that or she didn't rate female companionship very highly. She had been positively vivacious when monopolising Cal's attention the evening before.

'That old house is really something, but you need a man in it—even if it's just to pay the bills.' Ginger winked.

Sara smiled but refused to be drawn on the subject, making some comment on the surrounding countryside. A premonition of what her marriage would become haunted her and she was cool with Cal when he rose to greet her party at the golf club.

'All present and correct, sir,' she reported brightly,

noting the slight tightening of his mouth. She expected to be partnered with someone her husband wanted her to charm or alternatively someone he wanted out of the way, and was surprised when he drew her down on the leather seat beside him.

'I'm honoured.' She couldn't help the sarcasm that laced her tone. 'Which act is this? The happy couple?'

Cal's face was inches from her profile and she felt the warmth of his breath on her skin when he spoke. 'You know your problem?' he murmured. 'You got up too early.'

Walter Durkin broke into their private battle. 'Cal tells me you run the house as a separate business, Sara. I'd like to talk to you about that when you have a moment.'

'Certainly.' She was still too involved in recovering from her husband's remark to take in the implications of the request.

'I don't know if you've put him off or raised the price,' Cal growled, reluctantly amused as Durkin returned to his party.

'It's hardly the place.' Sara frowned and he shook his head, his eyes dancing with laughter.

'You need that course.'

Sara felt the sudden stiffening of his body and looked at him quickly. His expression was devoid of any pretence of charm, masculine aggression carved into every line of his face.

'Cal——?' she questioned him, and then she caught sight of Gareth.

'Sara!' He came over, his eyes holding the kind of pained joy she had only just begun to understand. How blind she had been!

'Hello, Gareth.' She smiled warmly, standing up and kissing his cheek. 'How are you? Stephen told me you were back. You certainly look well.'

'I got back yesterday.' His eyes feasted on her. 'You look wonderful.'

'Thank you.' She half turned. 'Cal, this is an old friend of mine, Gareth Haldane. He's just come back from Peru.'

'Interesting place,' Cal commented, getting up. Sliding his arm around Sara's shoulders, he extended his free hand to the younger man.

Gareth took it, his face hot and troubled. 'You're a lucky man.'

'Yes.' Cal tilted Sara's head back and viewed her face with detachment. 'I guess I am.'

'Why don't you join us?' Sara eased away without making it too obvious, disliking her husband's manner.

'We've got other guests, sweetheart. I think it would be a little ungracious if you spent all your time talking to Gareth.'

He sounded perfectly reasonable, but Sara felt her hackles rise. 'Yes, I suppose so, darling. Gareth, why don't you come to the house this evening? Around seven. We can chat for an hour before dinner.'

'I'll see you then,' Gareth glanced at the American, saw the possessive look he gave Sara and felt his insides catch fire.

'That was stupid,' Cal ground out, when the other man departed.

'Why?' She kept her tone low so she wouldn't be overheard.

He let his breath out in exasperation and picked up his drink. 'I can't believe you said that,' he muttered, a muscle flexing in his jaw. 'The guy's wearing his heart on his sleeve. You're mine, Sara, you'd better get used to the idea.'

'Oh, I'm yours, am I?' Her voice tinkled with ice as she let her gaze rest significantly on Bianca Shannon. 'And are you mine?' she queried sweetly.

'I provide the money,' he fended her off neatly. 'I like things clear. If you want anything else, you'll have to ask.'

Their eyes clashed like flints striking sparks. Stubbornness was something they shared. It was a long time before Sara looked away. When she did it was with a disdainful flick of her lashes that told him she wasn't prepared to be childish and turn it into a staring competition.

Later that evening, Sara fixed Gareth a drink in her private parlour. Serving her guest, she perched on the worn wooden rocking-chair.

'Tell me all about your travels.' She kept her tone light, trying to alleviate the weighty atmosphere in the room.

Gareth viewed her with a serious expression. Sara's delicate beauty had heightened to something almost exotic. Her black evening dress left her shoulders bare but for the thinnest of straps, her skin smooth and flawless except for a slight graze on her shoulder that, he knew with surety, was a mark of ownership from the detested Callum Grant. Sara moved restlessly. Realising he had been staring, he rushed into speech.

'I'm more interested in you, Sara. Quite a lot seems to have been happening here.'

'Yes,' she hedged. 'Of course, Daddy's illness was a terrible shock. He'll be coming home soon, and I'm sure St Clair's being revamped will take a lot of worry off his shoulders.'

'I'm sure.' He took a hasty gulp of his drink. To his eyes, the faded elegance of St Clair's had epitomised an England that had already slipped into the past. Something fine and pure that had faded from the world. In Sara he had longed to possess this elusive quality and preserve it. Instead, he was presented with a rejuvenated stately home and its mistress groomed and gleaming with Callum Grant's money. The pearl earrings and necklace, spun in a network of gold, cost a fortune. Even with his limited appreciation of female jewellery, he knew that. News of the St Clair's money problems had drawn him back home, with romantic visions of saving the woman of his dreams from ruin. His dream had turned into a nightmare. The American had taken his chance and managed to take on the multiple problems of Sara, her father and St Clair's without the slightest sign of getting entangled in the mess—the prediction his father had made for him when he had revealed his love for Sara. This added fuel to the flame.

'Callum Grant was a bit of a godsend. He can't be under any illusions about your motives. Doesn't he care that you don't love him?'

Sara smiled patiently. 'Daddy's illness undoubtedly speeded things up. We accepted there were risks involved in such a short relationship but it seems to be working.' Her eyes were compassionate. 'I know you're concerned about me, Gareth, but there's no need, believe me.'

All around them, photographs in silver frames

showed a past they both shared. Infant snaps of children's parties, church events, group pictures with their friends; it seemed to Gareth as if the wedding picture that should have crowned the collection had been distorted by some demonic subterfuge.

'I still love you, Sara. Dammit, I know you don't feel the same way, but if you had to have money, why couldn't it have been mine?'

'Gareth, please don't.' She felt terrible. She had always taken his affection for granted, never guessing the depth of his emotions. 'We can't be friends if you talk that way. Cal——'

'I don't care about Cal.' He was stubborn, almost sulking.

'Well, I do!' she said firmly, surprised at the amount of conviction her words carried. 'And you'd be foolish to cross him, he's a powerful man.' She regretted the words as soon as they were spoken.

'You're frightened of him,' he accused her with dawning realisation. 'Good lord, what does he do to make you feel like that?'

'I'm not frightened of him. You're being ridiculous.' Sara tried desperately to retrieve the situation. 'If you stay for dinner, Gareth, it's as my husband's guest as well as my own. I want us to remain friends; please don't make that difficult for me.'

Leaving the room, she let him make his own decision. She had to check that the final preparations for dinner that night were successfully under way. Perhaps it would have been wiser to ask Gareth to leave. Cal, she reflected darkly, would approve of that. Her life had become a juggling act, keeping the peace, originally between her father and Cal. Now, she had

Gareth's protestations of love and her husband's undoubted possessiveness to cope with. Life, she reflected, didn't get any easier.

Gareth stayed for dinner but his interest in his hosts showed less acceptance of the situation than his presence suggested. He manipulated the seating arrangements so that he was next to Sara and eyed Callum Grant with barely disguised contempt every time he spoke. Cal hardly spared him a glance but Sara knew him well enough to sense his anger.

She wasn't sure whether it was her imagination or Cal's deliberate intention to encourage Bianca Shannon that evening but the woman seemed to be permanently at his elbow. Bianca didn't direct her attention solely at Cal, but the shared glances and occasional private joke often drew them together to the exclusion of everyone else.

Ginger's mouth tightened and she cast an impatient glance at Sara. The fair Englishwoman maintained a politely interested air in Bianca's anecdotes, but something in her manner suggested she was bored, though far too well bred to make it obvious.

Cal's eyes rested on her for a moment and she arched an eyebrow in faint enquiry. She knew she was provoking him by her distant attitude but had little intention of revealing the hot seethe of emotions welling up inside her.

Bianca managed to annex the remainder of the couch Cal chose to occupy after the meal, curling her legs under her and draping her arm along the back-rest to ensure no one else joined them. Sara counted to ten.

'Bianca,' her voice was cool and even-tempered, 'I

know it's probably terribly old-fashioned of me, but I'd like to sit next to my husband.'

'Oh, sure.' Sherry-coloured eyes gleamed spitefully. 'I thought you English believed in correct distance, never touch in public and all that.'

'What a strange idea.' Taking the other woman's place, she brushed the fringe of hair that touched Cal's collar with one manicured finger.

Cal glanced at her briefly, before accepting a cup of coffee from Beatrice Pagett. His dark eyes were guarded, as if he wasn't sure of her purpose. Ginger Hailey, on the contrary, was delighted by Sara's unexpected show of possession, especially when achieved with such style.

'Do you find the English way of life a lot different, Cal?' Walter Durkin asked.

'I could write a book,' he growled, but smiled to take the sting out of his words.

'Americans are so much more direct,' Bianca claimed. 'They know what they want and they go for it. They don't pussyfoot around.'

'Life isn't always that simple,' Sara observed, ostensibly watching the vital black strands of hair fall back on to Cal's collar.

Putting down his coffee-cup, Cal casually put his arm around her shoulders, drawing her against him. His fingertips ran over the mark Gareth had homed in on, momentarily destroying his wife's cool superiority. 'The English enjoy complicating things,' he said, joining in the debate, his gaze roving negligently over Sara's face, his provoking attitude recognised by her alone. 'Life's about hunger and shelter——'

'Don't forget diamonds and good plumbing,' Ginger lightened the conversation.

'And if you can satisfy both needs in the same place, it's very convenient.' His voice was lowered so that only Sara could hear as the others laughed at the older woman's remarks.

Later, when they danced together, her husband abandoned the usual discreet distance and pulled her close. Sara had mixed feelings about his close proximity. Many women, she supposed, would be satisfied with the mixture of passion and possessiveness Callum showed her. She found it difficult to crystallise in her thoughts what she wanted of the relationship. She had vague images of long walks in quiet companionship, laughing at the same jokes. A hundred things that remained intangible but were recognisable in glimpses of other people's intimacy.

'Did he finally pluck up the courage to tell you how much he wanted you?' Cal kept Haldane in view while he spoke, his eyes insolently triumphant when they rested on his rival.

Fresh as she was from her reflections on the inadequacy of their relationship, anger made Sara's eyes intensely blue. 'Actually, he didn't mention wanting me at all. Hunger's all you understand, isn't it?'

His teeth showed in silent laughter. 'Wrapped it up in ribbons, did he? And what did you do, Sara? Treat him as if he'd got some kind of disease?'

She realised he was angry too and frowned. 'How would you like me to behave? You're my husband, Cal. My loyalty is to you.'

'Yes,' he breathed out softly. 'Well, I won't argue with that one.' Stroking her hair back from her cheek,

he rested his dark gaze on her lips. He bent his head
and kissed her firmly on the mouth. Her eyes were
closed when he lifted his head. Cal ran his thumb over
her lips, monitoring the ache of desire she was unable
to hide. 'I know you don't like public displays,' his
smile mocked her, 'but Gareth is beginning to annoy
me.'

Sara acquiesced to her husband's need to make his
claim on her with an unusual degree of tolerance,
fuelled by the fact that Bianca Shannon rarely took
interest in anything other than Cal. She endured endless fleeting touches that, while in no way indecent,
suggested to anyone with an atom of perception that
their host was still very much in the honeymoon mood.
She hoped their intimacy would convince Gareth that
she was serious about her marriage and, she grudgingly
admitted, warn off Bianca.

When Sara had the chance, she spoke to Walter
Durkin about his interest in St Clair's. Most of the
information she gave him was taken from the arrangements already made to accommodate the parties Cal
brought to the house. It occurred to her that it wouldn't
come amiss to have an information booklet designed
for conference groups. The businessman seemed quite
taken with the house and she promised to give him
further details. She would have to discuss what she
should charge with Cal, and find out on what dates he
wished to use St Clair's.

Going out on to the terrace, Sara breathed in the
cool evening air. The sky was grape-coloured, and the
night was damp, the trees dripping with water from a
recent shower. The smell of earth was strong after the
rain.

St Clair's was beginning to look like a healthy business proposition. It was wonderful what an injection of cash and the right contacts could do. Her father was coming home the next day to a future rosier than he could have hoped for. She owed that to Cal, she acknowledged silently. He had helped her separate the house's finance from her father's control in a way she could never have done. George St Clair lived very much in a man's world when it came to business. Cal's level-headed advice had had far more impact than her emotional appeals. Legally, she now held the reins of power; the entailment to Callum Grant's child was a private agreement that her father was in total ignorance of.

Her mind was active with unspoken questions. What was wrong with her? On the surface she had done rather well for herself. Practised gold-diggers, she reflected cynically, couldn't have done better. The only penalty clause was her marriage to Cal, and that could have been much worse. Perhaps it was old-fashioned to hanker after love. Gareth Haldane had offered her a gentle, romantic love and she had hardly noticed the agony of emotion he had suffered. It had taken Callum Grant's blatant masculine appreciation to make her aware of her own needs. He shocked her out of her 'strait-laced' complacency. The only rules he obeyed were those he considered contractual. He was scrupulous about those, she reflected darkly, remembering the abrupt cessation of their lovemaking that morning. Sara's fingernails pressed into the stone balustrade. When evening came, she felt almost sick with anticipation. Her skin was hot and cold in turns and she knew her eyes betrayed her feelings to Cal. He was adept at reading signs of female arousal. That evening, she felt particularly sensitive, wishing to postpone the enslavement of her senses as long as she could.

She was busily stacking the plates in the dishwasher when her husband found her.

'What are you doing?' he demanded in a low, thunderous tone.

'I told Mrs Pagett to go home. It won't take a minute.'

'Leave it until morning,' he instructed, pulling her away and undoing the apron she had put on.

'But in the morning they'll be——'

'Throw them away. Buy a new set,' he said between his teeth, clearly exasperated.

'Certainly not, they cost a fortune.'

'I don't care, Sara!'

Glancing at him quickly, she took off the rubber gloves she had been wearing. He was angry, she could see that in the hardness of his eyes and the tense lines of his shoulders.

'You're the perfect little housewife, aren't you?' he sneered. 'I sometimes think this is some giant doll's house and you're still playing Alice in Wonderland.'

His anger lit an answering flame in Sara. 'I wonder what that makes you.' She tried to move past him, only to be hauled back.

Glaring at him through a dishevelled wing of silver hair, she tossed her head back proudly. 'Why are you so angry, Cal? I'm sorry I got in Bianca's way but I thought it might be bad for business if her husband had to witness her flirting quite so openly with you.'

His fingers were painful, pressed into the soft flesh

of her upper arms, his dark eyes hatefully knowledgeable. 'You don't like Bianca.' His smile made her see
red.

'No, I don't like her,' she admitted honestly. 'She
puts me into the unpleasant position of having to
pretend I care about you!'

'How awful for you.' He drew her closer to him,
watching the colour come into her cheeks and the
panicked dilation of her pupils. 'So you don't mind me
taking up the lady's offer as long as we're discreet.'
Cal's hands slid up her arms to her shoulders and
pushed under her hair to cup her neck. 'Or would you
prefer to keep me in your bed?' His mouth brushed
hers. 'When you're hot and sweet, you're quite something.' His tongue licked against the mutinous stiffness
of her lips, his dark lashes lifting to witness the bitter
hurt in her eyes. 'Is it the first time you've felt jealousy,
Sara?' He kissed her hand, bringing it up to his cheek,
turning his mouth against it and biting gently. 'Not a
polite emotion, is it? I liked that little routine when
you ousted Bianca. Very smooth.' Taking her other
hand he raised them to his shoulders, his dark hair
brushing her pale flesh as he kissed the delicate inner
hollow at her elbow.

'I'm new to a lot of things, Cal.' She fought back
desperately; her resistance was slipping and she needed
to bolster it before she gave in to his seductive touch.
'Are you willing to turn a blind eye if I decide to follow
your example? I know modern marriages sometimes
have these arrangements——'

'No, Sara.' He was every inch the possessive male,
and the threat in his gaze made her flinch. 'Don't even
think about it.'

She winced at the grip of his fingers in her hair, a frightened cry of protest smothered as he rammed his mouth down on hers. Her fingers pushed against his shoulders, the dark cloth gathering up under her touch but not moving the hard bulk of his body. Her head dropped like a rag doll when he allowed her to escape the brutal kiss, the grip on her neck and the thumb under her jaw forcing her face upwards, making sure she understood. 'You're mine, Sara.' Dark eyes glittered angrily as he noted the vulnerable quiver of her lips. 'That's not negotiable.'

'Marriage isn't a business deal, Cal.' She was almost careless of the threat he embodied.

'Yes, it is.' He underlined each word with force. 'I own you. You belong to me. I want you to say it over and over again until you believe it.'

They both heard the approaching footsteps. Sara was glad of the reprieve, knowing that he was capable of making her utter those humiliating words. Swearing under his breath, Cal took her wrist firmly between his fingers, giving her a warning look as his grandmother came into the kitchen with the intention of making herself a hot drink.

'Not in bed yet?' She took in their disharmony at a glance. She said something quietly in Spanish which made Callum Grant stiffen and answer back with heat.

Prising her wrist free, Sara understood the threat in his eyes. If she left the house there would be hell to pay.

'Excuse me.' She smiled with an effort at Teresa Cortez, who seemed to approve of her tactical withdrawal. Cal was in danger of losing his temper, and it was something Sara had no desire to see.

She sought sanctuary in her private parlour. Trying to block Cal from her thoughts, she built up the dying fire, laying two medium-sized logs over the red embers. Watching the little yellow tongues crackle over the dry bark, she shivered. It was colder on the north side of the house.

What had possessed her to threaten him with infidelity? It was impossible for her to contemplate such a degree of intimacy with another man. It was Bianca, she acknowledged, her fingers pushing her hair away from her forehead in a perplexed movement. Cal knew she was jealous of the woman and had baited her with the fact. Pride had made her fight back. Unwittingly, she had opened the door for her own humiliation. Would Cal insist on a declaration of being his possession, his property? Her eyes were brilliant as they reflected the flames from the fire. So much for the cool poise she was universally credited with. She had every confidence in Cal's ability to elicit whatever he wanted from her.

The door opened. She didn't look up, the hairs at her nape stiffening as she heard the lock turn.

'We agreed this was my private room,' she began heatedly, flinching as the key landed close to her.

'I don't remember agreeing.' The clipped tone suggested his temper hadn't been cooled by his grandmother's interference. 'But when you were handing out terms, I seem to remember that during the night-time hours you were at my disposal.'

Standing close to her, with his hands in his pockets, he surveyed the photographs that had taunted Gareth earlier.

'You were a beautiful child.' He slanted a mocking

glance at her. 'I guess the big romance has been going on for some time. How serious did it get?'

'I've told you before——'

'Don't give me that,' he snapped. 'Haldane is sick with it. I know what it's like being near you and told not to touch. It's a game you play——'

'I do not play games!' She rose to look up into his face, feeling at a disadvantage kneeling on the rug.

'Did you kiss him?' He regarded her with heavy sarcasm. 'I doubt it got as far as heavy petting.' He deliberately smoothed the thin strap of her evening gown down over the curve of her shoulder. 'You wouldn't give any more than you had to. He doesn't do anything for you, does he, babe?'

Taking a shaken breath, she shook her head, unable to meet his eyes, staring desperately at the dark material of his evening jacket. His finger trailed over the rise of her breast, following the neckline of her dress.

'Haldane looks at you and sees all his dreams.' Sara's heart beat faster at the hypnotic sound of his voice, a cold tingle rushing to her toes as his finger traced her cleavage. 'Wonders what you look like when you're aroused.' The tormenting hand curved around her breast. 'Wonders what you sound like when you cry out.' Tightening his fingers momentarily, he relaxed them again, watching rebellious pride bring a spark to her eyes and the protest form as she parted her lips. 'And you smile and offer him tea. Politely ask if he enjoyed his exile in Peru.' His teeth glinted in his dark, swarthy countenance. 'And I could rip him apart for what he's thinking, because all this is mine.'

She twisted her face away, heat scorching her cheeks,

only to wince and meet his eyes as his grip on the small silver hairs at her nape made her attention a painful necessity. 'That's the truth of it, Sara.' He laughed softly at the mutiny written large on her pale features. 'And we both want it that way.'

Did she? Sara was confused. Cal described something raw and elemental. Hunger that spawned the ugly emotions of jealousy and possession. There was no denying she felt both emotions as strongly as he seemed to, but, whereas he considered her fidelity part of the contract between them, she had no say over his activities. Passion without finer emotions was a savage, destructive thing. It made her unhappy.

'Don't invite him here again.' Cal released her, his gaze unwavering as he tugged his bow-tie free from his collar. 'You can't claim innocence as a defence.'

Resentment flared in her eyes. She had no intention of encouraging Gareth. She felt guilty about the past but suspected that the fantasy image Gareth seemed to have of her was a million miles away from what she had become under her husband's tuition. Unwillingly she watched him opening the buttons of his shirt, swallowing drily, her eyes lifting to meet his, to drown in the dark sensuality there.

'You want me, don't you, Sara?'

The febrile glitter in her eyes told its own story. She endured the pure masculine assessment he subjected her to. Months earlier, she would have slapped his face.

'Yes, I want you.' Her voice shook. It was torture being so close: the scent from his body made her breathe in deeply, and she longed to reach out and touch the hard brown wall of his chest.

'Show me.' The brooding sexuality in his gaze melted her bones. Sara found she couldn't summon up anger or shame.

Unaware of how enchanting her confusion was to the man watching her, she let her hand slide under his shirt, his warmth and silky body hair exciting her. Moving into his arms, she pressed her lips against the bones at the base of his throat, her senses quickening as she felt his stomach tense beneath her caress. Cal's fingers combed gently through her hair, sure against the line of her spine as they dragged softly free of the tide of silver-gold and continued down her back. A langorous exchange of touch drew a sensual veil over the emotional violence of their encounter.

'Love is for poetry books. This is real.' His voice was rough with feeling. 'The rest is moonshine.'

Sara couldn't agree. The gleam of blue between her lashes showed that on that point she remained un-conquered. Her senses burnt away all thought of arguing as the remaining strap of her dress slid down her arm under her husband's persuasion. The black velvet gave under the insistent pressure of his fingers, the firelight glinting on the fantasy of gold and pearls around her throat.

'Cheap in comparison.' Cal released the clip, viewing the tanned skin of her upper chest, one finger tracing the paler area around her nipple, modest and yet incredibly erotic to the male who found every inch of her fascinating. Sara was disappointed when he chose to remove her earrings: her breasts had hardened in anticipation of his touch.

'You're a dream.' He let his hands close around the naked curve of her shoulders, bending his head and finding her mouth with blatant demand. Her eyes closed heavily as the kiss went on and on.

Cal's breath disintegrated as her caresses made him shudder, his spine damp, his embrace tightening painfully. Wriggling free, she pushed at the jacket of his evening suit, revealing the strong line of his shoulder.

'Cal, help,' she pleaded, and his mouth smiled but his eyes remained intent. Shrugging off his jacket, he obliged similarly with his shirt, accepting her half-hearted attempt at his cufflink, while her cheek brushed against the muscled build of his chest.

'I want you.' The words spilled from her lips in a litany, muffled as her mouth clung to the brown column of his throat, the tip of her tongue flicking over the vulnerable pulse that beat strongly there. 'It frightens me, Cal,' she whispered.

'Why?' His gaze took in the soft vulnerability of her mouth, reddened by his kiss as she tried to communicate her fears. 'The only time you need to be frightened is when you start to play around.'

Aroused as she was, Sara realised he'd said 'when' rather than 'if'. It occurred to her that he had an appalling view of the female sex, but she was distracted. Caressed and moulded by the sinewy strength of his hands, she felt sculpted anew. The wash of heat and cool air as his fingers swept over her shoulder-blades, spreading out over the plane of her back, finding the indentation of her spine and tracing it up to the nape of her neck, made her press against the hard wall of his body, her mouth open, tasting his skin with all the fervour of an addict.

Groaning, his mouth skimmed her throat, his lips hot on the creamy curve of her breast. Sara buried her lips in his hair, her fingers caressing his neck and shoulders, whispering his name as he circled the taut nipple with his tongue. Breathing deeply, she trembled as he took the hard peak into his mouth. Her knees felt as if they had turned to hot liquid, the fierce suckling sending shock waves throughout her body.

Cal's hands moved to her hips. Kissing a path down her body, he eased down on to his knees, his breath hot against her belly.

'I want you here.' He brushed her stomach with his lips, his eyes absorbed with her. 'I want to see your skin against the fur, see you naked in the firelight.' Mouthing her hipbone, he drowned his senses in her scent. Sara surfaced momentarily from the madness he wrought. Something was changing between them. Still unsure of this new world of powerful magic, she was distantly aware that they were breaking rules. This was her special place, he the intruder, and yet some instinct prompted her to follow where he led; victory did not necessarily go to the strongest.

'Sara.' He drew the lace briefs she wore down over her thighs, his features locked in a mask of hunger. 'I never know with you whether I'm master or servant.' Antagonism glinted in the depths of his eyes, his fingers flexing as his grip tightened at the top of her thighs.

Sara tossed back her hair, the blonde strands cascading back into place, catching the light and reflecting every shade from silver to the colour of honey. Sapphire-blue eyes were drowsy yet proud. She closed her eyes as hot kisses stung over her lower body. It was what she was made for, a seductive voice whispered as lightning ran along her veins. She couldn't be taken;

whatever his strength, Cal was paying homage to her womanhood in ways as ancient as man himself.

She was unaware of being lowered against the animal skin in front of the fire. Clutching Cal's shoulders, she held on to him as the only solid thing in a dissolving universe. She ached for completion.

'If you let another man touch you like this, I'll kill you!' Cal gripped a handful of her hair, his eyes narrowing, his lips parting as he joined their bodies. Their mouths met in a desperate need for assuagement, lips fusing as they followed the upward spiral of passion. Sara needed the night-time magic he wove around her. Cal drew her away from the convention and etiquette of her past, clawing away at the layers of history to a primitive truth that lay beyond. Rather than blame him for what he had done to her, she gloried in the mindless release of it all. At those moments, the cold light of day was as far away as the moon. She wanted to please him, to give him the beauty of her womanhood.

Sara's nails raked against the damp hair at his nape, the violent twist of fulfilment taking her almost beyond his control. Cal's head went back, the muscles of his throat strained as a spasm of pleasure shook him. His breath came in harsh pants, sweat gleaming on his upper lip and neck as his whole body shuddered. The muscles in his arms tightened as he tried to spare her his weight.

Sara remembered the threat when the golden haze of satiation began to drift away. Cal's arm was across her throat, his face very near to hers, black lashes spiking down against his olive-coloured skin. He felt her regard and opened his eyes fractionally, looking back at her. It was an exchange of mutual curiosity, as if they were staring into a mirror, seeing something they recognised in an alien dimension.

'I don't know why Gareth didn't carry you off on his white horse,' he commented lazily, quickly covering up the moment of communion. An idle finger pushed the hair out of her eyes. 'I'm just grateful I can do this for you and he can't.'

With an inexplicable feeling of sadness, she acknowledged Cal's limited emotional repertoire. She didn't hate him for it; it was a gap in his learning, like a missing word, a concept he didn't understand. Life was about hunger and shelter, and if you could satisfy both in the same place it was very convenient.

She went cold when she realised why accepting that was so hard. She loved him! Some malign cupid had sealed her fate, to love a man who didn't know what love meant.

'You're looking thoughtful again.' Cal levered himself up on to one elbow, leaning over to kiss the swollen curves of her lips softly. 'No woman has ever made me feel this good.' He slid his mouth down the side of her nose before returning to place small kisses under her lower lip.

Accepting the comfort of his embrace, she allowed the act of love to assuage the doomed hunger for the emotion he denied her. It was a fleeting comfort but one she couldn't resist.

CHAPTER EIGHT

SARA smiled fondly at her father as his eyes closed sleepily, glad to have him back at home after the weeks he had spent in convalescence. George St Clair looked well and more relaxed than he had been for years; she was glad she had been able to give him that sense of peace.

The mellow light of early evening sunshine warmed the conservatory, the palms and exotic blooms reminiscent of hotter, more distant climes. A path separated the conservatory wall from the row of clipped juniper trees marking the edge of the parkland. A huge copper beech swayed with majestic strength, leaves fluttering, molten bronze in the breeze. Everything breathed peace and stability. For her father and the others integrally involved with the house, that was true. The future had never looked more hopeful. Sara, on the other hand, had never felt less secure. Cal had been distant when they breakfasted together that morning. It was hard to imagine him making impassioned threats in the dark of the night, when he could begin the next day with nothing more pressing on his mind than the morning's post.

Mrs Pagett entered with a tea-tray and put it down quietly, dealing with the delicate china with an economy of movement that told of many years in service. Sara couldn't imagine Mrs Pagett knocking over a vase or dropping a tray. She wondered if the woman was happy. It seemed impertinent to even wonder about Mrs Pagett's emotional life after taking her for granted for most of her life. It occurred to Sara that she had rarely scratched the surface of life before Cal had arrived on the scene. It was odd that he should be the one to awaken her when he resisted any depth of emotion himself.

'Do you ever feel like breaking the lot?' She surprised them both by the question, and Mrs Pagett smiled.

'I think all newlyweds sometimes feel like that.' She attributed Sara's unusual question to marital strife. She was probably right; the frustrations involved in loving a heartless man were legion.

'Is Mr Grant going somewhere?' The question was asked innocently. 'Stephen Appleton is moving a lot of his files out of the study. He seems very busy.'

'I don't know.' She sipped at her tea, suppressing the desire to search out Stephen and find out what was going on. 'Something urgent might have cropped up.'

She doubted Cal would be insensitive enough to go without telling her, but business would override sentiment, she was sure. What sentiment? she chided herself. Cal's only emotion would be one of irritation that he had to find himself another bedmate. The thought made her go cold. Putting down the china teacup and saucer, she stood up, walking quietly past her father, and came across Stephen Appleton in the main hallway.

'You look busy,' she commented with a coolness she didn't feel. 'What's happening?'

He looked hot and rumpled, his jacket off and shirt-sleeves rolled up. 'Cal's got to go to New York. Didn't he tell you?'

The man himself saved her from answering, walking past them both, clearly not wasting any time.

'Come into the study,' he instructed, and Sara and Stephen exchanged glances. 'Sara,' he clarified, leaving the door open in his wake.

He was pressing digits on the telephone when she entered and quietly closed the door behind her. 'This is Callum Grant—get me Jerry Schafer, will you?' He spared Sara a glance as she came to sit on the edge of the desk, her profile averted from him. 'This has been brewing for quite a while. I shouldn't have left it so long.'

'Is it serious?' she asked, having very little idea about her husband's affairs other than that they took up a lot of his time.

'Depends what you mean. Some joker has messed up a deal I wanted; I'll just have to pick up the pieces. Don't worry, it won't affect you and Wonderland.' He waved vaguely to encompass the house.

'That's all right, then.' She was coldly sarcastic.

Reaching out, he tilted up her chin and frowned at the resentful glare she sent him. Sara almost hated him at times; he treated her like an employee with a vested interest in the business. That she would miss him never occurred to him.

'Do you want to come with me?' he asked in a rhetorical manner.

'I couldn't possibly leave St Clair's at such short notice,' she snapped back at him. 'Daddy's just come home and——'

'That's what I thought,' he cut her short. 'What's the problem? Has hot milk lost its appeal?' He grinned at the dirty look she sent him.

'I don't suppose you like it much, either.' She deliberately put her hand down on the phone, cutting off the call.

'What was that all about?' he asked with mock patience. 'I thought I'd paid enough to avoid the nagging wife routine.'

'I just think it would be courteous to offer a few moments of your time to explain to me where you're going. Do you know when you'll be back?' She kept her temper with an effort.

'No.' He was abrupt to the point of rudeness, equally irritated by her. 'I'll call you.'

'Why bother,' her voice was saccharine-sweet, 'when Stephen passes on messages so beautifully? I wouldn't want you to waste money on me, not when you'll be keeping in touch with Stephen anyway.'

He whistled silently. 'Your hair should have been red. That's quite a temper you've got.'

'I'm trying very hard to keep it under control,' she said between gritted teeth.

A malicious gleam in Cal's eyes warned her of further provocation. 'You know, honey, you're beginning to sound like a real wife.'

'I am a real wife.' She didn't care what he made of that, blue eyes spitting fury at him. 'It's a pity I haven't got a real husband!'

He picked up the receiver of the phone, giving her a warning look when she moved forward. 'Just go and find your lace hanky and wave me off. I haven't got time for your histrionics——'

The slap she administered resounded like a gunshot in the study and Stephen Appleton came in on it, looking from one to the other in an uncomfortable manner.

'Er—Schafer's on the other line in the drawing-room,' he offered as they continued to glare at each other. A smile tugged at his mouth, hastily flattened when Callum Grant's brooding gaze moved to take in his presence.

'OK.' He tugged his wife's hair in a mock-tease. 'Cool it, huh?' He followed Stephen out of the room and left her there seething, her palm tingling.

By the time he had left she had regained control of herself, or so she thought. Later, when tears trickled down her face and great sobs shook her body, she remembered how her lips had clung to his when he kissed her and the way he had gripped her shoulders and eased her away from him. So miserable was she that she didn't hear the door open, and she flinched as Teresa Cortez came close, a chocolate drink replacing the maligned glass of milk.

'Oh.' She scrubbed her cheeks with her fists. 'I didn't hear you.'

'That doesn't surprise me.' The old woman was dry but her eyes were kind. She shook her head, surveying the girl's tear-stained cheeks and bruised blue eyes. 'That grandson of mine. He thinks he has everything worked out, everything in neat little boxes until you kiss him, and then he runs off as if the devil's at his heels.'

'He was pleased to leave.' Sara sniffed and accepted a proffered handkerchief, blowing her nose and feeling too upset to pretend.

'Very probably. He's scared of you.' His grand-mother smiled at her disbelief. 'You don't think he's scared of anything, huh?' She chucked the younger woman under the chin. 'Well, he is. He's frightened of loving a woman in case he gets hurt.'

She sat on the side of the bed, searching through memories, her brown eyes saddened by her thoughts as she recalled the past.

'Maria, Cal's mother, set him a very bad example. She left James Grant when Cal was nine and I suspect only kept him with her to get her hands on the maintenance Grant paid for the boy. Cal adored her. The more she flitted in and out of his life, the more precious she became. When her husband died, Cal was fifteen and from then on I gave him a roof over his head when he needed it. She only contacted us when she wanted money. Cal stopped making excuses for her. He's never trusted a woman since, except his old grandmother, maybe.' Teresa Cortez's smile was weak. She passed the hot chocolate to Sara, her eyes kindly at the wide-eyed stare that attended her reminiscences. 'You should sleep; I think you might soon have more than Cal to think about.' She noted the young woman's startled realisation and nodded. 'Babies make women emotional. I haven't told him,' she answered the question in Sara's eyes. 'You must do that in your own time.'

Sara was silent for a moment, trying to come to terms with the fact that she was very probably pregnant and had been too immersed in her battle with her husband to realise it. It was hardly surprising, she reflected; they hadn't tried to prevent it and the frequency of their lovemaking made a baby inevitable.

A wave of protectiveness swept over her for both her husband and the child she carried. She and Cal both had painful memories from their childhood, bringing them to a premature form of independence. She had lost her mother; Cal to all extents and purposes had never had one. Sara was determined that their child would be brought up in an atmosphere of love and respect, and to do that things had to change in her relationship with her husband.

'I asked him about his mother,' Sara revealed to the older woman. 'He wouldn't tell me very much.'

'No.' Teresa Cortez looked grave. 'She lives in Florida. Cal makes her an allowance and she wastes it on shiftless young men who flatter her vanity.'

'I see.' Sara's face was pale, her eyes reflecting the deep sorrow she felt for the insecurity of her husband's formative years. 'Don't they ever see each other?'

She shook her head. 'Not often. Cal sometimes has to make a trip to sort out some mess she's got into. They always argue.'

Taking the empty mug of chocolate from her, Teresa tucked the covers around her grandson's wife, smiling at her fondly.

'I love him.' Sara couldn't keep it to herself any longer. Teresa Cortez might not know all the details of their marriage, but she appreciated the problems of loving such a complex character as Callum Grant. 'I don't think he wants me to feel that way but I can't help it.' Blue eyes beseeched the older woman. 'I don't know what to do.'

Surprisingly, Teresa chuckled. 'I think what you lack in experience, you make up for in instinct. Love him— he can't stop you.'

Put like that it sounded very simple. In practice, she knew it would hurt. It was a choice between showing she loved him or hiding it. Neither option promised a great deal of happiness.

Cal was away for most of July. If the days dragged, the nights were longer. Sara moved back into her own bedroom and found everything there childish. In a short-lived rebellion against the traditions embodied in St Clair's, she had had her room fitted out in white ash units. They were functional but looked antiseptic and sterile. Bookcases and chairs that bespoke modernism with their clean, geometric style didn't suit her melancholy mood. Anglepoise lamps and vases in poster colours suggested a clarity and boldness of youth that she no longer possessed. Sara was a woman passionately in love, with all the pain and pleasure that brought. Returning to the room she shared with Cal, she spent the night searching for his warmth, awakening fretful and racked by longing. She had to find a way through to him. Sara gazed at the ceiling, her naked limbs tangled in the sheets. The thought that he might be with someone else made her turn restlessly and bury her face against the sheet. She had to do something! But what evaded her.

Sara had a lot of time to ponder on the question of her marriage. She decided that Cal would never believe she genuinely loved him while she was in debt to him for saving St Clair's. The fact that she was having his baby would help convince him that her emotions resulted from a desire to play happy families. She hadn't much time, she concluded. Before long Cal would notice the changes in her body. She must act with speed.

Contacting an accountant who was a friend of the

family, she had him draw up a financial projection for the next five years for the house. The first draft was limited in detail, but she had enough to go to the bank and discuss a loan that would tide her over until the conference centre and restaurant put St Clair's back into the black. Walter Durkin's letter confirming block bookings for periods when Cal's firm weren't using the house made the venture look promising; so too did a sheaf of replies to the brochure she had circulated.

John Greaves, the bank manager, queried her desire for finance and she explained that she wished to make a go of St Clair's on her own, not have it seen as the hobby of a rich man's wife. This seemed to appease his curiosity and he agreed to the bank's financing the project subject to a more detailed projection being provided. Thus armed, she prepared for Cal's return.

Stephen Appleton informed her that Cal intended to return by private jet to Heathrow Airport the next day. 'He asked for you.' Cal's assistant saw the flare of anger in her eyes. 'You were out so I took a message.'

'Thank you, Stephen.' An imp of mischief sparkled in her eyes. Both men, she suspected, knew how she felt about go-betweens. 'I'll meet him.' She refused point-blank to be accompanied by Stephen or act as a courier. 'I'm sure you've dealt with all the urgent business on the telephone. Cal's spent enough time entertaining other people; he can take a night off.'

Airports, Sara reflected, had an ambivalent air of excitement, tiredness and the rather soulless quality of places of transit. She watched as passengers filtered through the VIP lounge and felt her heart jolt in her chest when her husband appeared, accompanied by his secretary Janice Chapman. The woman was in her fifties, super-efficient and very protective of her employer. Cal smiled at something she said and then his face sobered as he caught sight of Sara. Janice Chapman followed his gaze and smiled knowingly. Apparently, she was being met too, and waved at a grey-haired man who had just entered the lounge.

Cal surveyed his wife critically. 'You really throw yourself into the part, don't you?'

She ignored him and wound her arms around his neck, standing on tiptoe to kiss his cheek. Putting his hands on her waist to steady her, he returned the greeting, brushing his lips over hers.

'Do you have to wait for luggage or anything?'

'No, I travel light.' He indicated the holdall he was carrying. 'What happened to Steve?'

'Nothing.' She tucked her hand in his arm as they made their way out of the building. 'I thought a wife would probably want you to herself. She'd probably want to throw your paging machine out of the window too.'

'She would?' He considered this and then reached in his inside pocket and handed it over, amusement warming his eyes. His gaze moved over the cornflower-blue cotton skirt and top she wore and the baggy white jacket protecting her from the cool breeze.

One of the company cars awaited them and Cal slid across the seat beside her, resting his head against the leather seat, closing his eyes.

'Where are we going? St Clair's?'

'I thought we could spend the night in town.' She nodded at the driver and he turned the car towards the city.

'You're the boss.' He wound a strand of her hair

around his finger, his gaze resting on her lips. Her blue eyes darkened with the intensity of her feelings; Cal bent his head and they kissed deeply, breaking apart when the driver had to stop abruptly behind another car, reminding them where they were. Sara went pink and Cal grinned at her embarrassment.

'Spending the night at the apartment is a good idea,' he murmured into her ear. 'It's closer.'

'I thought we could go out.' She moved restlessly as he let his lips brush over her ear. It was typical of Cal to turn any show of warmth into an invitation to the bedroom.

'We could,' he agreed drily. 'It's up to you.'

She remembered her stipulation that their love-making should be a night-time affair and pondered on the dilemma that presented. She wanted to forget that silly deal. Glancing at her watch, she saw that it was only four o'clock. Cal followed the trend of her thoughts and laughed softly.

'Well, we could compromise,' he murmured. 'Do you want to go to a show?'

She considered the idea and nodded. Her social life had been restricted to entertaining his guests at St Clair's; it would be nice to go out without having to act as hostess.

'It's short notice to see any of the big shows. How about *A Streetcar Named Desire*; that's on in one of the smaller theatres?'

'We can see what you like,' he drawled, reaching for the phone in the car.

'I'd rather avoid crowds,' she demurred, not wishing to bump into anyone they knew.

He shrugged. 'It's your evening.'

They talked generally for the rest of the journey; he asked about George St Clair and his grandmother and she told him about St Clair's but kept her dealings with the bank from him, wanting the final details settled before she broke the news. The news of the baby would have to wait too, she decided with a pang; she wanted to give him her love undiluted by other ties.

She made coffee while he had a shower and made herself familiar with the apartment. It was only the second time she had visited the place. She liked it; it had none of the emotional or economic weight of St Clair's.

Cal came out of the shower, a towel wrapped around his waist, stretching lazily, the skin outlining his ribcage and drawing her eyes to the muscled strength of his body.

The Latin side of his nature had the upper hand when he was feeling romantic. She wondered if he knew how sensuality softened his features, how the dark lashes shielding his eyes made them so dark that to stare into them was like being absorbed into a dream.

His approach turned her limbs to jelly. Every nerve in her body went wild. 'The coffee's ready.' Sara attempted to pour the aromatic liquid.

'Thanks.' He noted her jerky movements. 'Put it down before you burn yourself.' He took the jug out of her hand and placed it back on the filter machine. Picking up the mug, he drank thirstily and sighed. 'I never have figured out why sitting still for a couple of hours is so tiring. Makes me want to go straight to bed,' he teased her, bending to see beyond the curtain of her hair. She gave him a hunted look.

'You haven't got a romantic bone in your body, have you?' she accused him.

He ignored this, placing a gentle kiss above her eyebrow and another against her temple. 'Does five o'clock count as evening or are you going to make me wait?'

'No.' She met the seductive brush of his lips with her own. It was pointless to deny the way she felt; his presence turned her into a mindless fool, and she needed to take the edge off her hunger to think straight. All her good intentions flew out of the window when they got into combat, and she knew he'd prefer to fight than explore the emotional depth between them.

'I don't want to wait,' she whispered, opening her mouth under his and winding her arms around his neck. His fingers moved through her hair, the silver-gold tresses washing silkily against his skin.

'Missed me?' He eased back, teasing her with a minimal movement of his mouth as hers begged for more.

'Yes.' Sara's eyes were confused as he tilted up her chin, his gaze raking her features.

'I missed you too.' He sounded as if the fact had been a revelation to him. 'It was a tight schedule, and when I'm working flat-out like that I don't usually need——'

'A woman?' she helped out, her eyes perceptibly cooling.

He noticed the change and frowned. 'I wasn't unfaithful, so you can take the ice out of your voice.'

'Why?' She widened her eyes naïvely. 'Didn't you have time?'

He looked uncomfortable. 'You're my wife. What do you think I'm going to do, look for the first available female?'

'I don't suppose you'd be the first,' she responded, irritated by the way he made 'female' sound like a convenience food. If he expected her to be flattered because he had wanted her rather than some good-time girl, he would be sorely disappointed.

'Oh, I see,' he said nastily. 'We're back to the hearts and flowers routine, are we? I suppose, because you've got to like the way I make you feel, you've convinced yourself you're in love with me. Yes, I thought so.' He looked amused by the thought, then slightly repentant when he saw the pain in her eyes. 'Don't worry, honey, it's a brief affliction. I've known women who fall in love on a monthly basis; they tear a page off the calendar every time a bigger bank balance appears on the scene.'

'I'm not like that, Cal.' She spoke with quiet dignity and he shrugged, uneasy with her emotional honesty.

'Maybe not—we'll see, shall we?' He released her and she watched him go towards the bedroom. 'We'll have dinner before we go out,' he informed her with a backward glance.

'I'd rather eat later.' She followed him. 'Didn't you have something on the plane?'

Unable to ignore her, Cal slowed and turned to lean against the door-jamb leading to the bedroom.

'Can't wait, can you?' he jibed, the hostile lines of his body emphasising the arrogant masculinity that claimed the right to instigate their lovemaking.

'No,' Sara agreed simply. Aware that he would rather return to the old battleground than tread new territory, she kept her temper. 'What difference will a few hours make? We'll still want each other and I will still love you.'

There, she'd said it! Sara didn't feel quite as cool as she sounded, but Cal's hunted expression showed that he had been fooled.

'Why the hell do you have to complicate things?' His hand clamped on her shoulder as if to ward her off, his exasperation expressed succinctly at the shadow of pain that crossed Sara's delicate features. 'People don't love, Sara. They bargain, they use each other, then they move on.'

'No.' She refused to accept his brutal assessment of human relationships. 'It doesn't have to be like that.' Funnily enough, the callousness of his rejection gave her hope. He was lashing out at her, trying to drive her away. Sara instinctively sensed she had to go through this fiery baptism to save them both from something much worse. Cal's first experience of love had been deeply painful; he had to be coaxed into trusting again.

He swallowed thickly as Sara let her hand caress his arm, her fingertips tracing the hardened muscle of his bicep.

'I taught you how to enjoy sex. I want no part in your schoolgirl fantasies.'

Blue eyes softly enticed him as she took his hand and kissed each finger with lazy brushes of her mouth before biting gently at the base of his thumb.

'Are you listening to me?' he grated, reluctantly captivated by her preoccupied expression.

'No.' Sliding her arms up around his neck, she met his brooding gaze with a simplicity of emotion that absorbed his anger and stirred something deep within him.

'You look so vulnerable.' The warmth of his breath feathered against her temple. 'But you feel dangerous.'

Sara pouted, tilting her head back to look at him. 'How can I be a danger to you? All you have to do is take. . .' Her words were softly spoken. The tension between them had undergone a subtle change.

Cal gazed at her intently. Such melting tenderness mixed with the cutting edge of hunger provided him with a myriad shifting contrasts. She had fought him proudly, surprised him at every turn, she fascinated and confounded him in a way he found maddeningly addictive.

'I'd hate to refuse a lady.' Taking the lapel of her jacket, he drew it off her shoulder, quite deliberately palming her breast and watching the conflict of desire and shock darken her eyes. 'I'm sorry, that was cheap.' He found he didn't want to drive her away and this time didn't fight it. She seemed to understand. His mouth found hers in a soothing caress. Again and again hard masculine lips returned to the giving softness of hers until their mouths fused in a fury of passion, the towel he wore falling between them, her cotton-clad thighs pressing against the muscled wall of his.

The hard, toasted brownness of his skin and the fresh male scent of him intoxicated Sara, her fingers urgently seeking out the ripple and mould of his muscles, finding a reality with him that stood in stark contrast to the grey days and nights endured in his absence. The sheer hunger in him made her ache. His loins impressed upon hers an urgency she matched, her skin tingling erotically under his touch.

'I suppose I should get you to bed.' Cal's eyes burnt over her as he freed her from the blue cotton top, the jacket already discarded on the floor. The lacy bra she wore enticed the heated search of his fingers, his eyes holding hers as the tips slid under the silken cup. Sara's eyes took on the drowsiness of a pampered Siamese cat, pleasured by its owner's caress.

'That look haunts me.' Cal bit at her lower lip, easing the nip with the stroke of his tongue, undoing the snap of the lacy garment and taking the full weight of her breast in his palm.

With a begging murmur, her lips closed on the tip of his tongue, inviting a deeper invasion which he responded to with devastating force. His arms tightened around her, binding her to him until the urgency of his need made him pick her up and take her into the bedroom.

A secretive smile touched Sara's mouth as she lived again the hour they had spent together. The warm bathwater silked against her limbs, the sensitised flesh heavy with languor. Before she had felt guilty about the satiation of her senses; now she found the memories of their lovemaking enveloped her in a pleasurable haze she was loath to break free from.

'Sure you want to go out?' Cal entered the turquoise-tiled bathroom, two glasses of chilled champagne in his hands. Dark eyes wickedly enjoyed her sudden confusion and he laughed at the guilty tide of colour that crept into her cheeks. 'Sorry, did I interrupt something?'

Despite her recent thoughts she found herself inexplicably uncomfortable with his presence in the bathroom, especially when he wasn't wearing a stitch. She lost the soap and covered up the moment of embarrassment trying to find it.

'Want some help?' Cal's lips brushed her nape, his tongue disturbing the small hairs that had escaped the topknot she had devised to keep her hair dry.

'I can manage, thank you.' The lazy way he was watching her made her feel the theatre was only a vague possibility.

'I can manage, thank you,' he mimicked, placing an extravagant kiss on her cheek. 'An hour ago, you were seducing me.'

'Get out!' She curled up her legs, her back ramrod-straight as he lowered himself into the bath.

'Never shared a bath, huh?' Cal pretended to be impressed. 'My upbringing made me more economical.' His toes deliberately smoothed against her thigh, enjoying her discomfort.

Knowing full well that Cal was reasserting his ascendancy made her meet his eyes levelly. 'You promised to take me to the theatre,' she reminded him.

'Mmm.' He watched her over the rim of his champagne glass. His dark hair was damp from the steam from the bath, the hair on his chest clinging in wet jags to his skin. Looking into his eyes was like experiencing a vivid flashback to the heady enchantment they had shared.

'Callum Grant!' she protested, a beautiful smile matching his slow grin.

'Tonight, I'm your slave.' He propped his head up on his hand, watching her as she finished bathing.

'I find that hard to believe.' She cast him a cautionary look, water gleaming on her body as she rose to her feet. Wrapping a towel rather self-consciously around herself, Sara stepped out of the bath.

'Why?' The small curls of silver hair at her nape and the pale gold of her skin absorbed him, the intimacy in his eyes stunning Sara into breathless immobility. She could find no light, teasing answer, and was both relieved and disappointed when he released her from his gaze, sinking down into the water with a sigh of contentment. Sara escaped; it was nearly more than she could do not to get back in.

Getting him to the theatre, later that evening, was a small triumph in their long-fought-out battle. For once they were just two people, enjoying each other's company with no other purpose than that. It was one of the few occasions when Sara had Cal totally to herself, outside the bedroom, and she wanted a romantic evening.

The curtains parted and Cal linked his fingers loosely through hers, the pale pink silk of her dress and matching jacket contrasting with the oatmeal-coloured cuff of his suit and thick gold wristband of his watch. It was a warm night and the thin cotton shirt he wore clearly didn't keep him cool enough; he tugged at the knot of his tie with his habitual desire to escape from its confines.

'What?' he queried her smile, his eyes indulgent.

'I don't know why you bother wearing ties,' she teased him. 'You always look as if you're at war with them.'

'I won't ever be a gentleman,' he admitted, without a trace of regret.

'Pity,' she said, manufacturing wistfulness. She smiled at him when he bent his head to see her expression, but his eyes remained guarded. Deciding that it wouldn't hurt him to be unsure of himself for a change, Sara bit back the reassurance that sprang to her lips.

The play was acted well and Sara thoroughly enjoyed the evening out. They went on to have a light supper at a restaurant. Sara refused a glass of wine and had orange juice instead.

Cal viewed her critically over the table. 'Sometimes I think you're too good to be true.'

She rested her chin on her interlaced fingers, giving him a direct look. 'How would you like me to behave? Like Bianca?' she suggested, keeping her voice level. 'You seem to find her amusing.'

His mouth twisted dismissively. 'If she were my wife, I'd strangle her,' he growled darkly. Picking up his glass, Cal regarded its contents reflectively. 'When you knock down walls between people, sometimes you can make a hell of a mess.'

Meeting the seriousness of his gaze, Sara's heart jolted with shock. He was warning her off, which meant the particular walls he surrounded himself with were in danger of collapse.

'Sometimes that has to happen,' she said quietly. 'Risk is part of life, you know that.'

'The words are easy.' He gestured to the waiter and asked for the bill, effectively finishing the conversation.

CHAPTER NINE

CAL reached out to find his wife, only to feel a kiss against his cheek that came from the side of the bed he was occupying. His lashes frayed apart and he saw Sara, fully dressed, regarding him with obvious amusement.

'What time is it?' He took the coffee she offered him and hung over it.

'Eight o'clock.' She sounded remarkably bright. 'I've been up since half-past five; you didn't notice me go.'

The demands St Clair's made on his wife didn't totally please Callum Grant, and he sprawled back among the sea of pillows, viewing the dungarees with disapprobation.

'I'm going to burn them,' he growled, smiling reluctantly as she pulled a face at him.

'You're very grumpy in the morning,' she offered as an observation, kicking off her shoes and shedding the dungarees.

'What are you doing?' He watched her as she unbuttoned the shirt underneath, his eyes lingering on the tanned length of her thighs.

'What does it look like?' She sat on the side of the bed near to him, undoing her watch. It didn't surprise her when he moved closer, drawing the shirt back from her shoulder, his mouth moving lazily against her neck.

'I thought you had an interview at the college this

157

morning,' he reminded her, making room for her as she pulled off the shirt and slid into bed beside him.

'I have, at eleven.' She let her hands slide over his shoulders as he leant over her.

'You smell of fresh bread,' he said as he breathed in the scent from her hair, his eyes dark and lazy as they met hers. 'Skin's cool.' He let his lips linger over hers, an indolent biting movement greeting the tentative touch of hers. 'I'll pick you up from the college and buy you lunch.'

'All right.' She smiled at him, pleased, and his gaze intensified.

'Sara, you know I can't spend all my time here, don't you? I work out of New York; I'll have to go back any time now. Developing the UK market is just one of the projects I'm working on. Before the year's out, I'll be handing that over to Steve.'

She looked troubled. 'And what exactly had you planned for me? You know I can't leave——'

'I can arrange it so that I'm based in London, but that's going to take time.' He avoided her gaze, pretending interest in a strand of her hair he was playing with. 'You're my wife, I want you with me.'

'Why?' she asked softly, putting a hand up to the side of his face to demand his attention. He met her eyes, his own dark and stormy with reluctant emotion. 'All right,' she whispered, kissing him placatingly. 'You don't have to say it.'

'Good.' He kissed her hard on the mouth. 'I know this place means a lot to you.' He closed his eyes as her fingers ran through his hair and she nuzzled his throat. 'I won't ask you to sacrifice that, but sometimes——'

'Mmm,' she agreed wholeheartedly. 'I miss you terribly, darling, but we'll work something out.'

'We'd better,' he growled, his mouth against her temple, moving to kiss her eyes shut before descending to the temptation of her lips. 'I've spent three weeks with hardly any sleep; it's a damn sickness but I can't beat it.'

Which was as near as he could get, Sara reflected later when she sat through her interview, to admitting he needed her. Cal hated being dependent on anyone. That hurt, but the week that had followed his return to London had been the happiest of her life. They had spent all their free time together and slowly Cal was beginning to relax his guard. It was like taming a wild stallion, she thought ruefully—that couldn't be done in a day.

The interview was merely a formality and she had the uncomfortable feeling that having a noted entrepreneur's wife as a student was a feather in the cap of the business studies department. She had hoped for anonymity; the unenviable position of being compared to Cal wasn't something she relished.

She bumped into Gareth Haldane on the way out, surprised to see him there. He explained that he was giving a series of evening lectures at the college in the coming term.

'Shall we grab a cup of coffee?' he invited, and Sara, wary of encouraging him after the episode at St Clair's, was glad to have a genuine excuse at hand.

'Actually, I'm in a bit of a rush——'

'Please, Sara.' He caught her hand. 'I have to talk to you.'

'No, I'm sorry, Gareth, Cal's picking me up.' She

glanced past him to see her husband mounting the steps. 'He's here now, excuse me——'

'Why keep up this sham?' Gareth Haldane turned to take in the American's approach. 'You're getting out of this preposterous marriage in your own quiet way. Why don't you smack him in the teeth with it? He deserves it.'

'I don't know what you're talking about. Please don't cause a scene, Gareth.'

Cal squared up to his would-be rival. The air fairly bristled with masculine aggression. 'Can't you find a woman of your own?' he snapped. 'She's my lady. I'm getting a bit tired of pointing that fact out to you.'

'Sara doesn't belong to you. You blackmailed her with her father's health, otherwise she wouldn't have taken your filthy money!'

'Really?' Cal pushed up the sleeves of the jacket he was wearing, the brown, muscular forearms revealed promising painful retribution. 'And where did you hear that fairy-tale? Sara loves me, don't you, darling? Tell the man and maybe we'll get some peace.'

Annoyed with Cal for treating her emotions as if they were public property, she hesitated for a fraction of a second and heard Gareth's hot words with horror.

'If she loved you,' Gareth burst out, 'she wouldn't be looking elsewhere for finance. Grenville's are backing St Clair's. She won't need you or your money!'

Sara was appalled. She had presumed her meeting with John Greaves was confidential. It had never occurred to her that her desire for independent finance could be twisted in such a way.

'You bitch!' Cal breathed out beneath his teeth. He

moved towards her and Gareth launched himself at the American, to be floored with one punch.

'Cal, please listen to me.' She grabbed his arm, glancing hastily at Gareth to see him sit up groggily. 'It isn't the way it seems. I was going to tell you.'

Black hatred mingled with pain blasted back at her. 'Very clever.' He pulled away from her as if he couldn't bear her to touch him. 'What were you waiting for? If you think you can twist the knife any deeper, you're wrong.'

'Cal!'

He held up his hands as she moved towards him. Bitter disillusionment scarred his features. The painful betrayal of his childhood washed over him like a dark wave. 'Keep away from me. I could dream away my life on your lies. I should thank him——' his finger stabbed in Gareth's direction '—for waking me up.'

Getting into his car, he slammed the door shut and the Mercedes roared on to the road. Sara watched it go with a frustrated, 'Damn!' and turned to look at Gareth's triumphant figure.

'I love Cal,' she said quietly. 'More than anything. I'm having his child. I don't think I'll ever forgive you for saying those things. I just pray to God I can convince him it isn't true.'

Gareth looked stunned at the blazing anger in her eyes and the sincerity of her tone. 'Then why seek finance elsewhere? He's loaded.' He rubbed his jaw, his eyes troubled.

'It's none of your business.' She walked over, extending a hand to him and helping him to his feet. 'But if it will satisfy your curiosity, we did make a hasty marriage. I wanted to separate the finances of St Clair's from our relationship.'

A crimson tide swept over Gareth Haldane's neck and face. 'I thought you had better taste than that, Sara.'

'And I never suspected you were such a snob. Or do you have to go to Peru before you can accept someone with a different culture?'

She left him standing on the steps of the college and hurried to the nearby market square where March Haverling's taxi rank would provide her with transport. Hoping that Cal would have cooled down and would at least listen to what she had to say, she endured the journey back to St Clair's. It didn't surprise her to find that he hadn't returned to the house, but when she failed to contact him at the apartment or the London office she was frantic with worry. Stephen Appleton appeared just as she was becoming desperate enough to call the hospitals and mentioned casually that Cal should be on his way.

'Where?' she pounced on his words. 'Where has he gone?'

Stephen frowned. 'Back to the States, didn't he tell you? The Hammond deal has gelled. He was keen to tie that up, so that he could take some time off. I thought he was going to meet you in March Haverling.'

'He did.' She sat down on the couch in the drawing-room, her attitude one of defeat. 'Could you get me the numbers of his apartment and office, Stephen? I'll call him later this evening.'

'Had a fight?' The young man grinned, having worked out the puzzle by himself. 'Not very good at goodbyes, are you? Last time you slapped him——'

'Just do as I ask and keep your opinions to yourself,' she snapped, feeling tired and upset and fed up with people interfering in her private life.

Worse was to come. When she eventually got through to his Manhattan apartment, a woman answered the phone who was quite clearly more interested in her companion than the person on the other end of the line.

'Darling, I think it must be the London office.' Sara slammed down the phone as she recognised Bianca Shannon's voice. What was she doing at Cal's apartment? You know what she's doing, she berated herself bitterly. Lord, he didn't waste much time! She was in little doubt that Cal intended to hurt her as much as she had hurt him. He succeeded; she spent the night alternatively sobbing and tortured by images of Cal and Bianca in each other's arms.

The weeks that followed were the most miserable of Sara's life. She ate mechanically in concern for the baby she was carrying and spent her nights in an agony of pain and hunger. The craving to see Cal, touch him, nearly drove her mad until anger at his emotional cowardice cauterised the wound and her heart hardened.

Teresa Cortez had left to visit relatives in Spain shortly before Cal's departure and she was the only one who knew of Sara's condition. It was fairly easy to disguise her pregnancy. She had a deep abhorrence of some concerned party's informing Cal of her condition and having him come back to honour his moral obligation. The bitterness that lay between them was a mockery of the security she wished for her child. And it was her child. Some part of Cal that he couldn't keep from her, some part of him that she could love and not be told she was foolish, dancing in moonshine.

Teresa Cortez's return upset the privacy she had enjoyed. George St Clair had revealed his worries about Cal's absence and the change in his daughter and Teresa, her gaze stern, found Sara in her private parlour.

'What has happened? Why isn't Cal here?' She came to sit beside Sara, raising her chin with an imperative hand. 'I thought everything was going so well. Poor child.' She recognised the pain Sara had thought vanquished. Blinking back tears, the younger woman told her the whole sorry tale, blowing her nose when she had finished and watching with suspicion as Teresa reached for the phone.

'No, please! I don't want him to know. He'll only come back——'

'He has to know, Sara.' Cal's grandmother was firm. 'You can't keep it a secret for much longer. Before long people will know you're pregnant and it won't take long to filter through to New York. Do you want him to find out from his staff? He won't like that, I can tell you.'

'I don't care.' She was mutinous but sat tensely while Teresa Cortez dialled the New York office. As it transpired, she needn't have worried. Cal it appeared had left New York on one of his walkabouts with Zac MacKenzie.

'Licking his wounds,' Teresa gave her opinion. 'He could be anywhere.'

Attempts to find Cal and Zac MacKenzie were made, but it appeared that Cal hadn't left an address or contact point. He had merely tied up any loose ends businesswise and left his business affairs to tick over while he disappeared from the map.

Christmas approached and Sara, now six months pregnant, had left the business of announcing her condition to her father and Teresa and carried on with her business course and running St Clair's, with a rest in the afternoon the only concession she made to her condition.

Planning the menu for the New Year, when the poultry and game were being prepared for Christmas, always gave her a feeling of time peculiarly concertina'd. It happened with every change of season, of course; once the spring menu was set, work began on the summer fare. She supposed there was nothing remarkable about her mixed feelings for the festive season, especially this year when so much had changed. Cal had claimed he would rescue her from an obsession with a pile of bricks. He had certainly done that. She had to force her attention to her tasks; it was no longer a labour of love. The house and estate approached Christmas with a timeless enthusiasm; her role was custodial and her mood didn't matter.

St Clair's luxuriated in an opulence that was no less attractive for the durability and practicality of the improvements. Holly bush, willow, ivy and mistletoe had been brought in from the gardens and were tastefully distributed. Log fires provided an attractive feature in both restaurant and coffee-shop. A local choir performed carols during the evenings and recordings were played during the day to create the appropriate yuletide atmosphere. Bookings for the restaurant and the opening of the coffee-shop for those who wished to stroll in the grounds had proved very successful.

Another of Cal's ideas, and she brooded on his continual presence in her thoughts.

Returning to the New Year menu, she attempted a light but mouthwatering selection that accounted for satiated palates suffering from the opulence of Christmas excess.

'Avocado soup,' she decided, discussing the subject with June Douglas. 'Devilled stuffed mushrooms. Fish, I think, rather than an emphasis on meat.'

'Prawns,' June added with relish. 'And clams. You're right. After Christmas, the roast definitely loses its appeal.'

'We can keep the traditional dishes, partridge, pheasant, that sort of thing, but the chicken and duck can go and drop the beef until the end of the month.'

June Douglas nodded, jotting down notes on her pad.

Sara was giving instructions about the tree decoration when Stephen Appleton came in with a rather sheepish-looking Gareth Haldane.

'Hello, Sara.' He glanced at Stephen. 'Can I—look, I'd like to help. Can we talk?'

Baffled, Sara indicated the study, and she was surprised when her father and Teresa joined them, looking from one to the other curiously.

'Gareth thinks he knows where Cal might be,' Stephen offered guiltily at her sudden comprehension. 'Well, I asked him to contact colleagues in the profession. It seems that Zac has been operating in the interior of Mexico.'

'I'll find him for you, if you want me to, Sara,' Gareth offered. 'I can't say how long it will take, but I'll try and get him here before the baby's born.'

Sighing, Sara went to the window, looking out into the sullen grey of the December day. What difference would it make? Cal's return would open all the old wounds, create the new pain of having to squabble over their child's future. Yet some sense of justice urged her that he should know. She couldn't bring his child into the world without giving him the knowledge of its existence.

'You can't not tell him, Sara.' Her father spoke gently. 'You know that.'

'Yes.' She turned back to them. 'Thank you, Gareth. Will you go with him, Stephen? I think he'd take it better from you.'

Stephen Appleton nodded. 'I meant to. I could do with some sun,' he added, trying to lighten the conversation.

The decision made, Sara felt oddly reassured. She hadn't contemplated the act of giving birth much but, when she did, the thought that her husband would be there took away the edge of fear.

The days and weeks, months dragged on. They heard from Gareth and Stephen when they reached Mexico but from then on they disappeared much in the same way Cal had. Sara didn't panic; in fact she was remarkably serene, convinced that she wouldn't have the baby until Cal returned.

She was in the kitchen when the first twinges began, and she sat down heavily on one of the wooden chairs. June Douglas came over to her quickly, ignoring the horn from the baker's van.

'What is it? Is it the baby?'

'I think so.' Sara was very pale, her eyes dark and wide with fear.

'Oh.' The woman visibly tried to keep calm. 'The doctor,' she decided, rushing towards the nearest telephone.

A car pulled up outside the hospital and three men, unusually tanned for the time of year, almost fell on to the wet paving in the rush to get out.

'Are you going to go in?' Stephen asked his employer, sounding a bit squeamish.

'I want to see her.' Callum Grant looked grim, his eyes sore and tired after days of continual travelling.

'It's this way.' Gareth knew the hospital from visiting his sister when she had had her first baby.

The receptionist on duty viewed them speculatively and Cal explained who he was. A nurse was summoned and took him to the theatre. He hesitated outside and she smiled.

'It often hits the macho types worst. You're not going to faint, are you?'

'No.' Cal was abrupt. 'I'm trying to summon the strength not to strangle my wife.'

'Oh!' The woman was startled. 'Perhaps it might be better if——'

'Just try and keep me away.' He pushed through the double doors and approached his wife slowly. The scene had elements of familiarity gained from fictional portrayals, but the calm movements of the staff were soothing. It was still a shock to see Sara, the swell of the child outlined by the white cotton smock. She turned her head, her eyes clouded with pain.

'Ah, the husband, I presume.' The doctor smiled in welcome. 'Everything's perfectly normal, shouldn't be long now. Did you get caught up in the traffic?'

Cal's short laugh was harsh. 'Something like that.' Taking Sara's hand, he touched her face gently. 'What's a nice girl like you doing in a place like this?' The humour didn't reach his eyes. Totally oblivious of those around them, he stroked his hand over her stomach. 'Do you want me to stay?' His eyes were dark and emotional.

A fierce contraction made her take in a deep breath and she clung to his hand. Sara didn't remember very much after that, only Cal demanding that the doctor give her something to make it easier for her and the medical man threatening to have him sent out if he didn't stop interfering.

After the birth she slept for hours in a quiet room, the baby sleeping in a transparent crib beside her. It was a boy, the thought penetrated the mists enfolding her. Wisps of black hair and eyes that were very dark.

When she woke, a strange sound came to her ears and she opened her eyes to see Cal with the baby up against his shoulder.

'They've got some baby milk in bottles, do you want me to——?'

'Bring him to me.' She had intended to feed the baby herself and a nurse came in, having heard the baby cry. Cheerful and giving practical instructions, she looked satisfied when the baby appeared to be feeding satisfactorily.

'Have you thought of a name?' she asked brightly.

Cal went to the window and stared out bleakly and Sara glanced at him.

'I'll get him some tea,' the nurse offered.

'Coffee,' Sara requested, stroking the baby's head absently. 'He hates tea.'

'Nice to know you remember something about me,' he offered roughly when the nurse left. 'Why in heaven's name did it take you six months to get round to the idea of telling me? Hell, I was lucky to get here in time as it was.'

'It didn't take me six months,' she murmured, absorbed with the baby's small features and feeling quite light-headed with relief that the birth was over and the baby was perfect. 'Disappearing to the wilds of Mexico didn't exactly make it easy to contact you.'

'You were pregnant before I left,' he accused her. 'I've been thinking back; you must have known in July. Your body changed.' His eyes swept over her breasts, stilling to watch the child tug at her nipple.

'I thought I'd call him Benjamin. Do you mind?' she asked, her cheeks taking on a pink tinge at his absorption.

'No, Ben will be fine.' He looked away, his hand going up to rake his hair. 'Looks like he's going to sleep. I'll change him and then you can rest.'

Taking the infant from her, he gently made the baby comfortable while she watched him. There was a slight tremor in his hands which he seemed to be aware of, his actions deliberately controlled.

The nurse returned, giving Cal the coffee, and nodded at the nappy. 'Quite a professional job. I think you should get some sleep, Mr Grant. Your friends tell me you've been travelling for several days.'

'It feels like it,' he admitted, drinking the coffee as if he needed it. Putting the cup down, he shoved himself away from the wall and approached his wife, sitting on the side of the bed. 'I guess this is all my fault.' He glanced sideways as the nurse left. 'Gareth apologised.

He told me what you said to him. It only needed one phone call, Sara; I wanted to come back so badly.' He groaned, burying his face into her neck. 'I love you so much, it's been hell without you.'

Sara put her hand up to the back of his head, stroking his hair comfortingly, feeling a distant compassion for his distress. She had made one phone call and found Bianca Shannon in residence. It would take time to know whether she could forgive and forget. Too much had happened within a short space of time to judge her emotions; she felt anaesthetised against all pain. It was a safe, emotionless cocoon, and she was reluctant to leave it.

Leaving the hospital wasn't the simple task Sara expected. A posse of journalists and photographers gathered at the main entrance. Callum Grant was news! The story of his disappearance and dash to his wife's bedside had got to the ears of the Press.

Cal listened to Stephen Appleton as he tactfully suggested it might be better to arrange a small Press conference and prevent a scrum as they left.

'No way,' he refused point-blank. 'I'm not putting her through that.' Looking tough and implacable in black jeans and grey knit shirt, leather jacket slung over his shoulder, he paused at the door to his wife's room. 'Make sure there's enough police cover. Sara needs some peace and quiet, not this damned circus.'

Leaving the younger man to attend his orders, he entered the room and took in the novelty of seeing his wife dressed after days in a nightdress and gown. A cherry-red suit matched with a white silk blouse provided a sharp, fresh contrast, and his son was newly attired in a blue jumpsuit.

'We have company, I hear,' Sara greeted him coolly.

'I should have expected it.' He picked up Benjamin, aware of the small frown knitting her brows at his action. 'I reckon we're going to have our son on the front page.'

'With some pithy phrase underneath.' She came towards him, meaning to take the child. '"Daddy's Home" springs to mind.'

'Why don't you suggest it?' He turned away, rubbing the child's back consolingly as the baby cried.

'Give him to me,' she fretted. 'He's not used to you.'

Cal's eyes were black with a mixture of pain and resentment. 'He's not going to be if you keep taking him from me. I am home and I'm staying. Got that?'

'You're making him cry.' She took Benjamin, watching her husband over the child's head, brushing her lips over the small, fluffy skull. A faint trace of guilt showed in the blue sapphire of her eyes. It was wrong to taunt Cal with her closeness to the child, but she found it hard to share Benjamin with him. He hadn't felt the wonder of the child grow. The baby hadn't existed for him for nine months as it had her. Underlying her reluctance was a shadowy awareness that Benjamin's very presence tied her to Callum, in a way that her father's health and love of St Clair's could never do. This frightened her; she dreaded the release of the floodgates of emotion that had previously wrecked her life and left her in this cold, withdrawn state. Even if it was true that Cal loved her, an ocean of pain stretched out between them as formidable as the Atlantic.

Cal's jaw tightened, his temper evident. He wanted to protect them both and she was deliberately excluding him. For the second time in his life he was vulnerable to the bitter mixture of love and pain that came from loving a woman, but this time he knew that much of the mess he was in was his own fault, and that was hard to cope with.

'Ready?' Stephen's head popped around the door. 'We've got enough police to form a tunnel to the car.'

A nurse took the child. Sara followed with Stephen behind her. A policeman came forward as they neared the glass doors.

'There's no danger of a stampede,' he reassured them. 'The worst of it will be shouting.'

'Stay close.' Cal turned to her. She nodded, taking hold of his outstretched hand. Several times her picture had featured in the local paper, due to some story linked with St Clair's. The full might of Fleet Street was something else again.

The noise was deafening. Questions spilled out from all directions. Had there been a separation. . .had the child brought them back together. . .had Cal gone to Mexico to get over the break-up of his marriage? Cameras seemed to be taking pictures from every conceivable angle. Sara glanced hastily at the back view of the nurse, relieved when the baby was given to Teresa Cortez waiting in the large limousine. Cal's arm went protectively around her shoulders, which excited a new wave of picture-taking. If anyone doubted Callum Grant's commitment to his wife, the barely harnessed energy he was willing to expend on anyone who harmed a hair of her head was a convincing testament. Sheltering in the arc of his arm, the blonde Englishwoman looked out at the zoo surrounding her and her eyes met his briefly with gratitude. Cal urged her into the car, looking across the roof as one of the loudest voices demanded a statement.

'Sure, I've got a statement. When I want the Press in my bedroom, I'll send you an invitation.'

Appreciative laughter greeted the comment and Cal got into the limousine, slamming the door shut.

The brief camaraderie their departure from the hospital engendered didn't last beyond the return to St Clair's. Cal's patience was severely tested in the weeks that followed the birth of their son. Sara was somewhere he couldn't reach. She sensed his frustration, but every time she softened she remembered Bianca Shannon.

She couldn't completely ostracise him, however, for Cal insisted on having the room next to hers. She tried to reach the baby as soon as he started to wake but physical exhaustion sometimes defeated her. When Benjamin's demanding cries wakened her the second time one night, she got up wearily and took him back to bed with her.

'Are you getting any sleep?' Cal tied his dressing-gown without any apparent haste or desire for modesty.

The sight of his sun-bronzed skin and hair-roughened chest made the room seem suddenly small and claustrophobic. Memories of the hard, masculine length of him moving over her in the most intimate of contact made her skin heat. She put the sudden stab of awareness down to embarrassment. She wished he wouldn't enter her room uninvited, especially when she was feeding Benjamin.

'You don't have to get up.' She drew the gaping line of her nightdress closer together, trying not to disturb the baby.

'If I change him and settle him down, you can get back to sleep. You're not getting up at some godforsaken hour for the baker, either. You're on edge, you need a good night's sleep.'

The look she gave him told Cal that his consideration was long overdue. He had given her endless sleepless nights, many more than their son. She agreed to his suggestion of tea to rid herself of his presence, noting thankfully that Benjamin's eyes had begun to close contentedly and that, although his mouth still moved against her, the urgency of hunger had abated. On Cal's return, she was easing the child from her, the creamy curve of her breast drawing Cal's unashamed attention when he reached out for the baby.

'You're in good shape,' he said smilingly as she pulled up the sheet in a swift movement. 'What are you hiding? I know every inch of you.' Dark, indolent eyes took in the hostility and resentment she didn't attempt to disguise.

'I can understand your being mad. . .' Her exclamation of disbelief made him look uncomfortable. 'You said you loved me,' he reminded her. 'You don't lie about things like that.'

'I'm tired, Cal.' She turned away, the light from the lamp outlining the curve of her shoulder and the shadow cast by her shoulder-blade. 'But I'm touched by your sudden faith in my honesty.'

Cal sighed with exasperation, taking his son back into the nursery and coming back when the child was asleep.

'Are you saying you don't love me?' He refused to let her ignore the subject any longer.

Wearily, she propped her head up with her hand,

meeting his gaze. 'I'm not ready for this kind of conversation, Cal. You'll just have to be patient.'

'And what is that supposed to mean? You've just had a baby. I was there, I know what it did to you.'

'It was a perfectly normal delivery,' she informed him, pleased that in one area of life, at least, she had greater endurance. 'Physically, I'm fine. Mentally, as far as you're concerned, I don't feel a thing and it's wonderful.'

'Well, I do. And I don't feel wonderful.' Her lashes flickered as he sat on the side of the bed. The intensity of his gaze engulfed her in a world of heated intimacy. She recognised his expression, she'd glimpsed it before in brief unguarded moments when they made love. Having revealed his love for her, Cal had dispensed with pretence. Had she not been packed in ice from his brutal departure from her life, she knew she would find him totally devastating.

'Don't keep pushing me away.' He reached out to stroke the curtain of hair back from her face, his hand warm against her cheek. 'I can make you feel better, Sara.' His mouth moved closer to hers, and she could feel the warmth of his breath against her lips.

'Planning on leaving?' She broke the spell his husky words weaved around her. For once she had all the cards, and she had no intention of relinquishing them to his soft-spoken seduction. It had been a mistake, she realised, telling him she had recovered from their son's birth.

'No.' He swallowed with difficulty, the defensive look in his eyes proving he understood.

'I don't need your money, Cal.' She maintained his

gaze. 'I don't even need your company to use St Clair's. The bookings are quite impressive.'

'I know.' He accepted the fact with ill grace.

'You're my guest,' she pressed home triumphantly. 'And even with your impressive wealth I doubt an English court would give you more than access to our son.'

'If you've got terms, let me hear them.' The bones of his face locked into a hard mask; he wasn't prepared to give in without a fight, she could see that.

'Terms?' She laughed bitterly. 'Back on familiar territory, Cal. You like it all written in black and white, don't you? Well, if that's all you understand, I do have terms, yes. Don't touch me unless I invite you to.' Later she tried to tell herself that the sinuous stretching movement that accompanied these words was merely an attempt to ease her cramped muscles. 'Do you understand?'

Cal's lip curled in cold humour. 'Perfectly. But it's only fair to point out, that provocation and invitation are pretty much the same to me. And when you move like that——' his hand swept with insulting familiarity from her breast to her thigh '—the difference escapes me.'

'Get out!' she whispered fiercely, her composure destroyed.

'Just as long as we understand each other,' he mocked her, standing up, his figure a dark shadow in the room as he moved out of the light.

Sara's heart beat a tattoo against her ribs long after his departure. He should be at a disadvantage, she fumed. She had meant to teach him a lesson. How had Cal turned the tables on her? The unwelcome response of her flesh to his touch made her groan. 'Not again,' she pleaded, the word whispered against her pillow. 'Please, not again.'

Cal refused to oblige her by removing his presence from the house. He worked mainly from St Clair's, occasionally visiting London, and from what Sara gleaned from Stephen Appleton was transferring his power centre to the capital. St Clair's was prospering as a conference centre, the experience earned from the first year invaluable. Angela Carter had been drawn into the enterprise and, together with Sara's deputy, June Douglas, allowed Sara to delegate many of the chores binding her to the house. It seemed rather ironic that, as Cal transferred his interests to London, both her father's health and the running of St Clair's placed fewer demands upon her.

Benjamin's christening prompted a meeting over coffee in the conservatory. Fragile April sunshine shone through a glitter of raindrops suspended on the glass, the aromatic smell of coffee scenting the air.

Cal was already seated, talking to Stephen, who Sara imagined was there purely for the coffee. The two men had become good friends; the dash from the interior of Mexico had been a turning point in their relationship. Stephen had matured from the self-seeking shark he had appeared a year ago and had a new air of responsibility about him. Gareth Haldane had taken up a teaching post at Oxford and was consoling himself with the more than willing Angela, who, despite her blasé attitude to life, appeared quite smitten.

'Shouldn't Benjamin be here?' her father joked. 'After all, he is the subject under discussion.'

'Bring that young man in here; his cries are loud

enough to break the glass,' Teresa Cortez offered with an element of pride. 'Takes after his father.'

Sara glanced over at Cal to find him lazily appraising the picture she made in the crisp shirtwaister dress. She had been pleased with the renewed trim lines of her figure, and the white dress with a waist-pinching blue leather belt had been worn in a celebration of the fact. Cal's appreciation, she maintained stubbornly, had been the last thing on her mind. Ignoring the seat next to him, she went to the other side of one of the cane tables, sitting with her team, comprising Angela and June.

'Benjamin's sleeping.' She gave Cal a suspicious look when he personally brought her coffee to her.

'Strange,' he murmured, capturing her gaze with his dark glance. 'If I got as close as Ben, the last thing I'd want to do is sleep.'

Sara pretended to study the guest list, ignoring his comment, but from the broad grin on Angela's face she presumed his voice had carried at least that far, and she felt the colour stain her cheeks.

Her eyes narrowed as one name leapt out at her from the printed list in front of her. All it took was the sight of Bianca Shannon's name to release the love, passion and jealousy that had been battened down since Benjamin's birth.

'If you think that woman is staying in my house, you can damn well think again!' She flung the guest list at Cal across the breakfast table, much to the surprise of all assembled.

'Sara——' Her father looked shocked at such an outburst but the others, a little more tuned in to the tensions between the pair, sensed that the lull was over and that the storm needed to clear the air was about to break.

'You'll have to be more specific, darling.' Cal regarded her angry features calmly. 'Who is it that you object to?'

'Take a wild guess,' she invited, blue eyes electric. 'You can put your mistress up at a hotel and save me the humiliation as well as the expense.'

'My mistress?' He cast his eye over the guest list and Sara pushed her chair back, his mild but firm, 'Stay where you are,' freezing her in mid-action. 'It's not the charming Bianca, is it?' He raised an eyebrow, his eyes gleaming at the sheer fury she embodied.

'Why? Who else did you have in mind?' she spat out furiously. 'Is there more than one?'

'Sara, really!' George St Clair looked most uncomfortable and Cal cast him a glance.

'If you'll excuse us,' he got to his feet, 'while we clear up this little misunderstanding? Some kind of post-natal fantasy, I expect,' he goaded her, watching her go up in flames with grim satisfaction.

'It's not fantasy.' She stood up, her hands on the table. 'Just one call, you said, and you'd come back. Well, I made that call, I wanted to explain about Grenville's financing St Clair's, but *you* didn't answer the phone, Bianca Shannon did.'

Cal's mouth hardened noticeably. 'Why didn't you wait to speak to me? Bianca Shannon was staying with her husband at my apartment. Their place was being redecorated. I wasn't alone with her and, if I were, it wouldn't make any difference. In case you haven't noticed, I happen to be crazy about you.' His sudden awareness of their audience made him come around the table and grab her wrist. 'If that's why you've been giving me such a hard time, my opinion on the subject is definitely not for public consumption.'

'Get off.' She tried to pull free, still angry but wanting to believe him at the same time.

'No.' He was unrelenting, and as soon as they were out of the conservatory he hoisted her over his shoulder in a fireman's lift, leaving her to flail at his back with her fists and view Mrs Pagett's unbelievably smiling countenance from her topsy-turvy position.

'If Ben cries,' Cal instructed as he mounted the stairs, 'give him some of that powdered milk. His mother is going to be otherwise engaged for some time.'

'How can you be so selfish?' she gasped, rescinding his order to what she felt were deaf ears.

'Very easily.' He reached the bedroom and kicked the door shut when they were inside. Dumping her on the bed, he took off the jacket of his navy suit. 'I've spent nearly a year without you. And why? Because Bianca Shannon, a woman whom I personally despise, answers my phone.' Undoing his tie, he regarded her angrily. 'It's interesting that, while I'm supposed to endorse your candidacy for sainthood, you tar me with the morals of a sewer rat!'

'I have no pretensions to being a saint,' she almost yelled at him. 'And the tactics you used to get me to marry you were no better than those of a sewer rat. I don't know why I love you, you haven't one redeeming feature.'

'Yes, I have.' He undid his shirt, his gaze softening at her admission of love. 'I don't let you get your own way. I'm the only male you've ever acknowledged as an equal.' Cal moved closer to her and reached out to touch her hair, aware of the dying fire in her eyes. 'You can be yourself with me. Be weak, be strong— angry——' his thumb brushed her lips '—passionate, loving and totally beautiful.'

A startled comprehension that he fully intended to end their estrangement flooded Sara's body with a sweet longing, calming the rush of heated accusations that had seemed so important moments before. Closing her eyes, she acknowledged her need of him with a soft sigh, the last breath of her temper.

'I've been so lonely without you,' she admitted, lifting stricken, vulnerable eyes to his. 'I never intended to hurt you, Cal. When the money was between us or even the fact of my getting pregnant, you were always going to think I was just making the best of things.' Tears trembled on her lashes. 'I wanted to repay the money I owed you. It was a gift, not an act of betrayal.'

Raking back his hair, the raw, tense, aching look in his eyes undisguised, Cal said, 'Blackmailing you into marriage wasn't exactly a good basis for a trusting relationship. You made it clear you wanted out at the first possible moment.'

'I told you I loved you,' Sara whispered. 'I broke that damned contract I insisted on. It hurt when you laughed at the way I felt, made it sounded cheap or. . .or my way of making my desire for you respectable. You never let me love you the way I wanted to.'

'Don't, sweetheart.' Cal knelt on the bed beside her, pulling her against his chest. His mouth found the softness of hers and he kissed her with a deep reverence. His tender caresses adored the pink, vulnerable tremor of her lips, his fingers entwined in the tangled silk of her hair.

'I wanted you to love me,' he whispered huskily against her throat. 'I just couldn't believe that you did—that it would last. I was too busy arming myself for when it would end. I knew it would hurt so damn much if it did.'

'Oh, Cal.' She held him tightly, willing to forgive him anything, knowing that his lack of trust had come from harsh experience in an unhappy childhood. 'Teresa told me about your mother, so I do understand. If it hadn't been for Bianca. . .'

'You have nothing in common with either of those two *ladies*.' He used the term with laboured politeness, stroking her hair back from her flushed cheek, a muscle clenching in his jaw at his own stupidity. 'When I first saw you at the casino, I should have known that. Beauty can easily be bought, but not integrity.' He groaned wryly. 'I don't deserve anything from you. If it hadn't been for your father's illness, you would have avoided me like the plague.'

Sara wasn't totally convinced. The attraction between them was a powerful force. Even now, when he spoke, the warmth of his body so close to hers drew her touch, her pale fairness a direct contrast to the deeply bronzed skin beneath her fingers, the dark hairs forming a cross on his chest abrasive against their tips. Sara's eyes burnt with the blue heat of high summer when she lifted her gaze to his face.

'Maybe I did something right.' His eyes darkened, his breathing thickening with excitement as Sara wound her arms around his neck. 'Sara.' His arms tightened fiercely around her. 'Lord, when you look at me like that. . . You're so damned innocent about it. I swore you'd never drive me to the extremes Haldane took but I couldn't take being near you without this.' His mouth moved over hers in a barely restrained need for assuagement.

Sara couldn't believe the explosion of feeling his touch brought. His words might have filled her with a feeling of female triumph when the battle still raged between them, but victory would have been hollow. Cal's pride would never have allowed her to humiliate him, however smitten he was, she had proof of that from the night she had forbidden him to touch her. In the battle of the sexes only a draw could bring satisfaction.

No longer guilty about her sexuality, she revelled in every movement of his muscular body. Cal's heart hammered against her breast, his urgency conveyed as he changed their positions so that she lay beneath him on the bed, his larger frame swamping hers, his arm moving to help her to take his shirt off. Tearing his mouth from Sara's, Cal closed his eyes, trying to gain strength as her lips covered his face in kisses.

'Are you sure this is OK?' His lashes parted to show a hot, barely restrained demand.

Running her fingertips along his broad shoulders, she murmured, 'Perfect,' the provocative purr in her voice deliberately misunderstanding him.

Cal's intent gaze showed he was beyond such gentle teasing. 'I'm fine,' she admitted, her heart in her eyes, lashes closing over a shimmer of blue as he bent his head and kissed the skin exposed by the V of her dress. To give herself up to the shattering intimacy she shared with Cal, she needed his love to protect her against the pain and jealousy such nakedness of emotion could engender. Quivering with excitment, Sara held her breath as he stroked his hand over her breast, the crisp cotton abrasive against the silk-covered nipple hardening beneath his touch.

'It's been so long.' His voice was jagged and raw. Tugging the buttons free, he groaned appreciatively as she bit lovingly at his neck. 'I don't want to hurt you. I need you so much. . .' Capturing her mouth, his burning kisses made them move restlessly against each other, until Sara melted back against the pillows, leaving herself open to his pleasure. Drawing the material over the rise of her breast, Cal slid the silky cup of her bra back from her skin.

'Oh, darling,' she whispered, as he traced the curve of her breast, his tongue caressing one of the darkened peaks. The gentle torture went on, the swollen globes of her breasts cupped by his strong brown fingers.

'I love you,' he groaned, rubbing his face against her soft warmth, 'so much that it aches in me.'

Sara knew all about that, whispering her love to him. Her eyes closed as his lips wandered restlessly over her face, possessing her mouth, his tongue sliding silkily against hers, his fingers undoing the blue belt around her waist, flattening his hand to caress the renewed tightness of her belly.

With hot, trembling fingers Sara unfastened the clip of his trousers, needing the naked strength of him against her. Pushing her dress down over her waist, Cal showed a similar determination, their bodies twisting together, the hot sting of flesh against flesh demanding fulfilment. Cal's hard frame pressing against the softness of Sara's brought a fleeting relief.

His gentleness was a testimony to the depth of his feelings but Sara, driven by the needs of unfettered womanhood, drew him deep beyond the bounds of thought, into a realm of passionate intensity that left them entwined in each other's arms, totally drained, after the long months of emotional torment.

It was dark when they lay together side by side, kissing occasionally, physically satiated, enjoying just being close.

'Married, with a child,' Cal drawled, his dark eyes caressing her. 'I never dreamt being so respectable could feel so good.'

'Did you really need a wife for business purposes?' Sara asked, kissing his jaw lingeringly. She felt secure enough not to reflect on his less than respectable interludes.

'It seemed like a good idea at the time.' He subjected her to a lazy appraisal. 'You would never have considered anything else, would you? I could tell that from your conversation with Stephen out in the gardens at Ravenswood.'

'You were insultingly direct in your attentions,' she pointed out, her lashes closing to give him a narrow-eyed stare. 'I disliked you intensely.'

'I know.' He rubbed his thumb over the base of her chin, regarding her with deep warmth and amusement. 'You were so proud, so squeaky clean, I wanted to mess you up, smear your lipstick, run my hands through your hair, make you look the way I was feeling.'

Her eyebrow arched in amused enquiry.

'Hot,' he growled against her lips.

A familiar wail, loud and indignant, disturbed the peace of the night.

'I think I've got competition.' Cal kissed her breasts, his eyes laughing into hers. Getting up, he went through to the nursery. 'Here she is,' he crooned to the child, sitting down on the side of the bed, his eyes protective as he settled Benjamin against her. 'He's like me, isn't he?' His finger touched the back of the small dimpled hand splayed against her flesh, the Latin skin-tone darker. 'I meant his colouring.' He gave her a chiding look.

'Yes, darling.' The warmth of his regard was heavenly to Sara.

'We both need you very badly. Do you think you can handle two demanding males?'

'I think so,' she murmured provocatively, stroking her son's wispy hair but her eyes resting on her husband. 'If I can cope with you, the rest is easy.'

Three women, three loves . . . Haunted by one dark, forbidden secret.

ALIX ATKINSON

Boundaries

Margaret – a corner of her heart would always remain Karl's, but now she had to reveal the secrets of their passion which still had the power to haunt and disturb.

Miriam – the child of that forbidden love, hurt by her mother's little love for her, had been seduced by Israel's magic and the love of a special man.

Hannah – blonde and delicate, was the child of that love and in her blue eyes, Margaret could again see Karl.

It was for the girl's sake that the truth had to be told, for only by confessing the secrets of the past could Margaret give Hannah hope for the future.

W●RLDWIDE

NEW AUTHOR SELECTION SURVEY 1991

Spare a few minutes to tell us your views about our
NEW AUTHOR SELECTION for 1991,
and we will send you a

FREE Mills & Boon Romance
as our thank you.

Dont forget to fill in your name and address, so that
we know where to send your FREE book!

Please tick the appropriate box to indicate your answers ☑

1 How did you obtain your NEW AUTHOR SELECTION?

Mills & Boon Reader Service .... ☐

W.H. Smith, John Menzies, another newsagent .... ☐

Boots, Woolworth, Department Store .... ☐

Supermarket .... ☐

Received as a gift .... ☐

Other (Please specify) _____

2 If you bought the pack for yourself, what made you choose it?

_____

_____

3 If the pack was a gift, who bought it for you?

_____

4 a) Which of the four authors did you enjoy the most?

_____

b) Why? _____

_____

5 Do you intend to read more Romances by the author that you enjoyed the most?

Yes ☐   No ☐   Not sure ☐

6 a) Which of the four authors did you enjoy the least?

_____

b) Why?_____

_____

7

Would you like to make any other comments about the New Author Selection?

_____

_____

_____

8 How many Mills & Boon Romances do you normally read?

Less than one a month ☐   Five to ten a month ☐

One a month ☐   More than ten a month ☐

Two to four a month ☐   Other (please specify)

_____

9 What is your age group?

16 – 24 ☐   35 – 44 ☐   55 – 64 ☐

25 – 34 ☐   45 – 54 ☐   65 plus ☐

Thank you for your help ── **NO STAMP NEEDED** ── NAP91C

Please send to: Mills & Boon Reader Service,
FREEPOST, P.O. Box 236, Croydon, CR9 9EL.

Mrs. / Ms. / Miss. / Mr. _____

Address _____

_____

_____

_____

_____ Postcode _____

You may be mailed with other offers as result of this application. If you would prefer not to share this opportunity please tick the box ☐

ASSOCIATION OF MAIL ORDER

mps *MAILING PREFERENCE SERVICE*